INDIGO ISLAND

INDIGO ISLAND

SUSAN MOORE

nosy crow

First published in the UK in 2018 by Nosy Crow Ltd
The Crow's Nest, 14 Baden Place
Crosby Row, London, SE1 1YW, UK

Nosy Crow and associated logos are trademarks and/or registered
trademarks of Nosy Crow Ltd

A CIP catalogue record for this book is available from the British Library

Printed and bound in the UK by Clays Ltd, St Ives Plc
Typeset by Tiger Media

Papers used by Nosy Crow are made from wood grown in
sustainable forests.

ISBN: 978 0 85763 9585

www.nosycrow.com

For Richie, Jodi & Gary

FUTURE TECH AND OTHER COOL STUFF

BATCAN: A robotics factory specialising in hybrid robots. Founded by Lang Liu. Headquarters – Kowloon.

FASTPAD: A flexible, tough, wafer-thin tablet computer, which can be rolled up. Invented by UK-based technology company Fenomenell.

GROOVERIDER: A low-slung, hydrogen-powered sports car with a distinctive grooved bonnet. Designed and manufactured by Choprider, Shanghai.

NEWSAMP: A 24/7 news service delivering ranked, hottest news stories.

OCTOZEB GOGGLES: Diamond-def, virtual-reality goggles designed and made by SPIN, Hong Kong.

OVERRIDER: A super-sized, six-wheeled all-terrain truck. Originally developed for the Chinese army by Choprider, Shanghai.

PHEROWIFF: A type of robot sensor that can detect pheromones.

POPKO JUICE: A range of juice smoothies served in striped layers containing a secret Popko ingredient.

ROCKETBOAT: A hydrogen-powered, cigar-shaped speedboat, capable of rapid acceleration and speeds of up to 300 kmph.

SLAMBURGER: The ultimate Yanbian beefburger created by top Hong Kong chef Shen Slam. Shen's signature toppings are legendary, with Slamburger winning Best Hong Kong Burger (voted for by Big Dragon News) for the last five years.

SLIDER: A skateboard-shaped, electrically powered hover board with pop-up handlebars. The Slider was invented by Beijing Bikes' top engineer, Liu Lee, using the same principles of motion as the classic hovercraft from the twentieth century. Sales of Sliders have outstripped bicycles by four hundred per cent over the last two years.

SMARTSHEET: Wafer-thin, everlasting digital paper.

SMART T-SHIRT: An e-textile T-shirt containing soft, flexible screens on the front and back for display of movie clips, photos or text.

SPIN: The world's largest virtual-reality games company. Designers and builders of three bestselling games – "Empire of the Shadow", "Want of Truth" and "Lavanter". Founded by Max and Catherine Walker. Headquarters – Hong Kong.

URBRUN: A US sports company that makes running suits with neon-lit active seam technology to maintain optimum muscle performance.

V-STYLER: A hydrogen-powered, top of the range private jet, with speeds of up to 1,000 kmph

WARZWORLD: Virtual-reality games company with fully immersive war worlds ranging from Aztec kingdoms to Alien planets. Players must be certified 18 to play. Founded by Baroness Ivy Shiversand. Headquarters – London.

WRISTER: A wristband with embedded smart-payment technology used by market traders and taxi drivers.

Chapter One
FLYING HIGH

The jet rocketed through the ink-black night on its way to San Francisco. Nat pressed her cheek up against the window. She couldn't see a thing outside, but the smooth glass cooled her skin. She closed her eyes and for the hundredth time willed it to go faster. It was a V-Styler, the speediest private jet ever made. It was fully tricked out – VR bed seats, everlasting velvet carpets, a Stewbot butler. Despite the luxury, she would much rather be on the ocean on the *Junko* boat. Being in the sky in a jet like this only reminded her of how her parents had died, all those years ago.

"Are we nearly there yet?" she said.

Her dragon robot, Fizz, was resting against a purple velvet cushion on the seat next to her. He was deep in sleep, getting a full power recharge before they landed. He'd switched on his light-snore mode so that he sounded like a purring cat. The moment he heard her question, though, his eyes snapped open.

"*Forty-eight minutes,*" he reported.

"Rat's tails! I bet that slimy Zixin is ahead of us now. For all we know he could already have the sword."

Fizz ruffled his wings. The tiny emerald scales shimmered like leaves on a bright spring day. *"He and his scheming snake, Vesperetta."* His long sigh was followed by a wisp of white smoke, which came curling out of his long, green snout. *"Vesperetta..."* he paused, shoulders slumping. *"I was wrong to trust her."*

Nat couldn't be bothered to reply. They'd talked about this a thousand times. She was stupid to have trusted Zixin when she had met him at school back in London. He was like a cunning fox. All that "I'm just a poor East End boy" had been a lie, and she'd believed it. He'd stolen the Mo Ye sword and disappeared off into the mist in his kayak. *"Nice work, heiress. Here, let me help you with that,"* he'd said, taking it from her. *Ai yah!* How stupid she'd been. She could kick herself for trusting him. And now he was after the Gan Jiang sword too. She had to beat him to San Francisco and find it before he could.

"Henry, go and get changed before we land," said a voice from behind her.

Nat turned to see Aunt Vera leaning over her cousin, Henry. She'd changed into a scarlet and silver striped

Shan-xi dress with matching stilettos. A whiff of her freshly sprayed Super Spice perfume wafted up the cabin. Nat wrinkled her nose. She'd rather stick her nose in a pair of old socks than inhale that oily stink.

"Ouch! Stop it!" shouted Henry.

Aunt Vera was trying to tug off his Octozeb goggles, but Henry kept batting her hands away. He'd been in virtual reality for the whole flight, along with his robot squirrel, NutNut. It was perched on the arm of his seat and had been wired in so long that its soft brown fur was all standing on end, making it look twice its normal size. Nat guessed Henry had probably got them into the Lavanter winter world, a new destination in the SPIN gaming universe. Once in there they'd never want to leave.

"Behave, Henry!" screeched Aunt Vera, wrenching the goggles off his head. "Or I'll pack you off to reality camp!"

Henry scowled at her. His eyes were bloodshot and he'd got dark patches of goggle shadow around his eyes.

"Go, wash your face, brush your teeth, and put on the suit I've left for you in the bathroom."

Henry didn't move.

"NOW!" she screeched again, startling him like a deer.

He leapt out of his seat and ran for the bathroom at the back of the jet.

"*Your guardian is on the rampage*," said Fizz.

"Excuse me!" said Aunt Vera, spinning round to where Nat was sitting.

"Wasn't me," said Nat, shrugging.

Aunt Vera pointed a long, freshly-painted nail at Fizz. "How rude."

Fizz's eyes flashed red. "*I am not rude, it is a fact. You are on the rampage, but you must excuse me for the error I just made. I should have addressed you as temporary guardian.*"

Aunt Vera snorted like a bull and came marching up the aisle, her bracelets jangling. Nat reached over and plucked Fizz out her reach. Things were bad enough as it was, she didn't need more drama.

"Well, little dragon, I assure you that it is only a matter of time before it becomes a permanent arrangement."

Fizz wriggled in Nat's grasp, trying to free his wings, but she held firm. A long orange flame shot out of his snout. Aunt Vera leapt back.

"No flames on board, Fizz. You'll set off the

alarm!" said Nat.

Aunt Vera looked at Nat. If the Cementer face-smoother she used would allow her skin to move, she would have had frown lines across her forehead like a ploughed field.

"I will not allow you to step off the jet dressed like that!"

Nat flinched as a long scarlet-painted nail stabbed the air between them.

"Imagine if someone sees you and publishes a photo of you! You are the heiress to SPIN. When Henry comes out, go to the bathroom and have a wash. I'll put one of my dresses in there for you."

A flashback of the terrible days spent living under her aunt's rule back in Hong Kong sparked fury in Nat. "*Zoinks!* I am not going to put on one of your *un-ku*, Shan-xi schmancy dresses again in a zillion years!"

Aunt Vera pursed her lips into a sort of thin smile. "As your guardian I demand that you do. If you defy me I shall forbid you to leave the hotel."

She spun on her spiky heel and marched off up the aisle, snapping her fingers in the air. "Stewbot, come here at once and arrange my hair!"

The robot butler came whizzing out of the galley

kitchen, its two wheels spinning silently along the velvet floor.

"If Stewbot has any sense, it'll take its laser torch to that mushroom hairdo of hers," said Nat, relaxing her grip on Fizz. "Is there a 3D printer onboard?"

Fizz flew over to where a polished wood desk unit was built into the cabin wall. He used a silver talon to activate the control panel on the top. "*Affirmative,*" he said.

"*Ku.* Have you still got the clothes designs that Wen sent before we left?"

He nodded his snout up and down. Nat hadn't looked at what her best friend had sent her from Hong Kong, but they had to be better than whatever horror her aunt had in mind.

Chapter Two
MAKEOVER

The bathroom door opened and Henry walked out dressed in a blue blazer and a white shirt with grey trousers. He might only be eleven but he looked like a mini-version of his dad. Nat had to bite her lip to stop herself from giggling.

"Hair," said Aunt Vera, grabbing him by the sleeve as he walked by.

Henry's hand shot up to try and smooth down the mass of red, bed-head hair that hadn't been touched since he'd come on board.

"That won't do at all. Sit down there!" She pointed to the seat across the aisle from her.

Henry frowned, sighed and followed her orders.

"Stewbot, go and cut Henry's hair."

"*Yes, Mrs Walker,*" the robot said, giving her hair one last blast of hairspray, before wheeling towards Henry.

"No way. I am not having my hair cut!" said Henry, getting up from his seat.

But before he could stand up, Stewbot's white-gloved, metal hands shot out, pushed him back into his seat and strapped him in using the seat's full harness. It whipped a SPIN logo napkin out of a pocket, whisked it around his neck, activated its "scissor-hands" setting, and set about chopping his hair.

Henry squirmed, trying to break free, but the harness had him pinned.

"Natalie!" called Aunt Vera.

"*Pssst. Down here!*"

Nat looked over to find Fizz underneath the desk using his talons to push out a shiny, grey box that was three times his size.

"*This is it*," he whispered.

She stepped over and picked it up. It wasn't small enough to get past her aunt unnoticed so she grabbed the cashmere blanket off the back of her seat and bundled it up. "*Zoula!*" she said.

Fizz flew up on to her shoulder. She rushed up the aisle, ignoring Aunt Vera's glare, bypassing the Stewbot who was still at work on Henry's hair, and locked herself in the bathroom. She put the loo lid down, unwrapped the printer and sat it on top.

"Print out everything that Wen sent, please."

Fizz swooped down from her shoulder and hit the

power button. "*Connecting now,*" he said.

The cartridges and spools inside whirred and ratcheted. Nat turned to the mirror over the washbasin. She looked pale, her chin was spotty, and the dark circles under her eyes made her look a hundred. The old purple kung fu jacket she was wearing was frayed at the cuffs. Behind her, on a hook, hung a red and yellow stripy Shan-xi suit. If she put that on she'd look like the mustard and ketchup topping on a hotdog.

"Fizz, I need you to help me."

He hopped up on to the marble counter top, and perched on the edge of the washbasin.

"*Your wish is my command, my lady,*" he said, with a bow.

"Mum was from San Francisco. She always looked *ku* in all the old photos, so I want to look good too. Make me look like Natalie Walker, daughter of Catherine Walker."

"*I've never done a makeover before.*"

Nat crouched down so that they were eye-to eye. "Now's your chance to show me who you think I really am."

Fizz cocked his head on one side and blew out a thin trail of white smoke. "*I must not disappoint you.*"

Nat laughed and pointed at Aunt Vera's dress. "Anything you do has to be better than that!"

Fizz turned, clacked across the marble on his talons, opened the mirrored vanity cupboard and climbed inside. She watched the tip of his scaly tail flick from side to side as he rooted through its contents.

The printer pinged. A dark blue collar began to appear in the output tray.

"*Miss Walker, please take your seat for landing,*" announced the Stewbot, tapping on the door.

She glanced at the Shan-xi dress. No way.

"*Highest chance of success if you sit down,*" said Fizz, reappearing with bottles, brushes and tubes.

"You'll have to be quick, we're landing soon," she said, kneeling down on the tiled floor.

"*Please close your eyes and I shall begin my work.*"

She did as she was told. Whatever he did, it couldn't make her look worse than she did now. She could feel first cold, then warm brush strokes across her face and neck.

"*Miss Walker, I must insist that you return to your seat immediately!*" announced the Stewbot, rapping hard on the door.

"Hurry!" she whispered.

"Nearly complete. Don't open your eyes until I am done."

She could feel his talons moving through her hair. "What are you doing?"

"Working my way through a Crowflick hair tutorial at ten times normal speed."

The printer pinged again.

"I will need to use my authority to open the door and escort you back to the safety of your seat, Miss Walker," said the Stewbot.

She heard its spring-filled body start to extend towards the door lock.

"Coming, just finishing on the loo, don't come in!" shouted Nat.

The noise stopped. She opened her eyes. Fizz whisked a dark blue Slider jacket and leggings off the printer tray and handed them to her. She tugged off her old jacket and pulled on the new one. It activated. Nat smiled. Wen had uploaded a short clip of them both in their Kung-fu gear on the mats at Ken's studio in Hong Kong. They were armed with bo-sticks and were taking it in turns to practise their moves on a wooden dummy. Ken had allowed them to dress up the dummy as their arch enemy so that they could channel their inner warrior ... so it had a mushroom wig on top and was wearing a pink and white striped Shan-xi dress that Aunt Vera had once forced Nat to wear in Hong Kong.

"Miss Walker!"

The Stewbot again. She pulled on the leggings, stuffed the old clothes into the rubbish bin and grabbed the printer off the loo. She turned to the door handle but stopped dead in her tracks when she caught sight of herself in the mirror.

"You like my work?" said Fizz, from his perch back on her shoulder.

Nat blinked and leaned closer to the mirror. She must be seeing things... Her hair was no longer its usual red colour, it was now a deep indigo blue with a zigzag fringe and heavy chopped layering. Her eyebrows matched. Fizz had fixed on false silver eyelashes, and covered her skin in a thin layer of pale Cementer. Her cheeks were shaded to accentuate her bone structure.

Nat smiled. Nothing could stand in her way when she looked like this.

The latch snapped back, the door flew open and the strong, gloved hand of the Stewbot grabbed her arm and pulled her out of the bathroom.

"Ku!" said Henry, catching sight of her as she

stepped into the aisle.

Aunt Vera let out a bellow. "There is no way you're going into the United States of America dressed like that!"

Chapter Three
BONDING

Zixin could hear his grandad's voice shouting inside his head.

"Enough sleep. Time to get up. Time to find Gan Jiang! I must have that sword!"

He forced himself to lift his leaden eyelids, hoping it was all just a nightmare and that he'd wake up back in his bedroom at home in London. Instead, he was blinded by a spotlight shining directly in his face. His pillow had vanished. He put his hand down to push himself up off the narrow guest bed above Hong's shop, but instead of a soft, cotton sheet, his fingers met with thick plastic.

"What time is it?" he mumbled.

No reply. He moved his hand to the small of his back. It was the place where his robot snake always lay, coiled up in sleep-mode, ready to activate when his day began. There was no familiar, warm chain-linked form. The space she occupied was cold.

"Vesperetta, come here."

INDIGO ISLAND

This jet lag was terrible, it felt like someone was hitting his head with a hammer.

"Take it slowly, my boy. Easy does it."

His grandad's voice was coming from inside his left ear. He lifted his hand to the side of his head. As he did so his fingers met with a cluster of long, hedgehog-like spikes. The moment he touched them an electric shock zapped through his head.

"Ahhhh!" he screamed, pain exploding through to the roots of his teeth.

"No, don't touch there. The needles haven't finished their work."

Another hand batted his away and held it down on the plastic. It was that sharp voice of Hong, his grandad's old friend. He'd met him the night before when he'd arrived. He'd still yet to see his grandad, though.

The pain dulled. Zixin opened his eyes again. This time the spotlight was gone. In its place was Hong, complete with surgical face-mask.

"He needs more time to adjust," he said.

Adjust? To what? Cold, clammy fear gripped Zixin's guts. He looked past Hong to find that he'd been mysteriously moved from the room where he had gone to sleep to the medical couch in the acupuncture consultation room. The smell of pine disinfectant in the windowless, grey-walled room made his stomach heave.

"What have you done to me?" he said.

"A little adjustment, my boy. A family bond has been formed."

Again, his grandad's voice was coming from inside his left ear. He wrenched his wrist from Hong's grasp, rolled off the couch, and came to a wobbly standing position. It was like being at sea. He was swaying from one foot to the other, and he felt like throwing up.

This whole trip he'd been forced to make was one bad thing after another. He'd rather be at school, bored at the back of the class, or bored in the dingy flat with his dad in London, than be here in San Francisco.

He lifted his arm, wrapped his fingers around the handful of needles and pulled them out.

"No, not yet, too soon!" said Hong, shaking his head, eyes wide behind the thick lenses of his glasses.

A buzzing sound started to fill Zixin's ear.

"WHAT HAVE YOU DONE TO ME!" he screamed.

The agony propelled him. He had to escape. He took Hong out with a swift side kick, knocking him to the tiled floor. But before he could reach the door it flew open. Scorta, his grandad's guinea-lion robot, came racing in with a ferocious roar. It pounced on Zixin, pushing him to the floor and pinning him down with two massive furry paws.

"*Don't you dare hurt Hong!*" squeaked the guinea-pig face shooting out of the giant lion body.

Scorta nipped him on the cheek.

He'd seen these kind of hybrid creatures in virtual worlds before. WarZworld was full of half-man, half-dinosaur avatars, but this one was real. Laughter exploded like a firework in his head, but it wasn't his own.

"Nice kung-fu kick, my boy, but keep those moves for when we really need them."

"GET OUT OF MY HEAD!" screamed Zixin.

More laughter.

"We're bonded. Proper family now. I can guide you, help you navigate to places where I cannot go. Together we will find the sword and conquer the world!"

Zixin writhed under Scorta's paws, trying to break free, but the guinea-lion still had him pinned.

"Hong has kindly implanted a nano speaker and recorder deep in your ear so that we can communicate at all times," said his grandad.

"Why can't you just go and get the swords yourself?"

His grandad sniffed. "I'll show you why."

Zixin heard the flapping of wings both in his ear and coming from the corridor. Seconds later a giant eagle came swooping into the room and landed on the couch. What he saw next made his head spin so much that he did throw up, all over Scorta's paws. His grandad's wrinkled, bald head was stuck on the giant eagle's body. He was half robot. No wonder his grandad had never shown himself on screen when he'd called. He was a living freak. And why an eagle? Couldn't he have just got himself sized up for a humanoid-style exoskeleton?

Zixin vowed to escape, go to a hospital and get them to remove the implant, then he'd go to the airport, get the next flight to London and leave this nightmare behind. He just needed his snake.

"Where's Vesperetta?" he said.

"She's a very interesting creation," said his grandad.

The way he emphasised "creation" made Zixin's blood turn to ice. Vesperetta was his only friend. She was his snake buddy.

"What have you done with her?"

"I have been examining her. My findings are that you

have the same skill for robot design and construction that I do. I would have expected nothing less. I am still better than you, of course, but for a first attempt, your snake is not bad."

Zixin stopped struggling. Scorta lifted its paws off him and sat back on its haunches, staring at him, its beady guinea-pig eyes unblinking. Examining? Had he taken her to pieces?

"Where is she?"

"She is in a safe place."

"I want her back, now."

"Now? Oh no. Not possible. I fear she will detract from our bonding. Once we have found both swords, she will be restored to you."

A pain tore through Zixin. It was far greater than the physical agonies of the nano implant. It was the pain of separation from the only thing he'd ever loved.

"*The girl is about to land,*" announced Scorta.

Chapter Four
SAN FRANCISCO

The pilot banked to the left. Red strands of dawn came streaming in through Nat's window. From where she was strapped into her seat she could see the Golden Gate Bridge glowing in the distance.

The sun was bathing it in light, making it look like some magical gateway to a mythical land. To the right of the bridge San Francisco rose up, a mixture of skyscrapers, office blocks, wooden houses and flats clinging to its undulating hills. To the left lay the lush green mountains of Marin.

This was it, she was about to land in the city where her mother had been born. She'd only been here once before. Her parents had come over from Hong Kong on a visit to see her grandfather, but she'd only been a baby then. Now she was fourteen and on a mission to find the ancient sword Gan Jiang before anyone else could lay their hands on it.

Finding the first sword, Mo Ye, had been much easier. The ghostly form of her mum had appeared in the special SPIN game that her dad had created for her and told her that Mo Ye was hidden in a cave in Cornwall. To find Gan Jiang, all she had to go on was a cryptic message delivered by the character of an old witch whom she'd met the first time she'd played the SPIN game.

The message was handwritten by her mum – she recognised the curve of her arty lettering – and simply said: "*You must do what your father and I couldn't: find Gan Jiang in San Francisco.*"

That was it. Nat had thought her mum might have given more of a hint about where to start searching, but after Zixin had managed to hack into her game and find the message too, she understood why – the hackers were everywhere. Zixin was probably already down there somewhere, busy searching. And maybe there were others too, waiting for her. A chill ran down her spine. Danger lurked everywhere.

The jet touched down and taxied into the private plane zone at San Francisco airport. They stepped out into a clear, blue-skied day. The air was sharp and clean with a salty taste to it. A customs and immigration official met them at the bottom of the steps and swiftly stamped them into the country, before escorting them to a waiting stretch-Grooverider.

So this was America. Nat had seen it in the movies and in virtual worlds, but this was the real thing.

Old-fashioned, chip-fat fuelled yellow cabs stood in a line against the sidewalk. Super-sized Overriders were being loaded with suitcases and people. The Slider lane was chockablock with luxury, wide boards of the kind that were banned from the narrow Slider lanes of London and Hong Kong. Most of the riders were dressed in Goldrush cowboy style, wearing jeans, spurs, check shirts and ten gallon hats.

The Grooverider motored like a stately grey whale on to the freeway. Traffic was heavy and they crawled along at a snail's pace. Aunt Vera sat purse-lipped, behind massive dark sunglasses, drumming her fingernails on the walnut drinks cabinet while sipping whisky from a heavy crystal tumbler stacked with ice cubes. Henry sat next to her. He had fallen asleep after his marathon gaming session on the jet and was using NutNut for a pillow, his head squashing the squirrel up against the window.

Nat and Fizz sat opposite. Nat was still defiantly wearing her Slider jacket, playing the kung-fu clip. She looked at her aunt, then reached inside her jacket and pressed the power down button. The kung-fu scene disappeared.

Aunt Vera managed a thin smile. "Thank you. I will not ask you to change clothes but I do request that you don't play that again."

"Done," said Nat.

An eyebrow arched over the top of the glasses. "We have a deal, then. I would also appreciate you acting like we are a united family when we check in at the hotel. I do not want to wash any more of our dirty laundry in public."

Nat nodded. She didn't want that, either. They were a newsworthy family. She'd learned that from an early age when NewsAmp had headlined: *"Maverick gaming creators and SPIN founders, Max and Catherine Walker, tragically killed when jet turns into fireball mid-flight."* Ever since that tragic day, reporters were always on her case. Her late guardian, Jamuka, had kept her below the radar. Rich families with problems could feed the news headlines for days.

"My oh my!" said Aunt Vera, pointing towards the windscreen. Nat turned around to look. The Grooverider had moved off the freeway and was headed down a ramp into the city. San Francisco fanned out before them in a mishmash of skyscrapers, brick warehouses, glass office and apartment blocks. Some were short, some tall, some wide, some narrow.

It was like Hong Kong, but on a smaller scale.

"I'm not sure I like this Goldrush style. It looks so rural," sniffed Aunt Vera, as they headed downtown.

Nat watched a group of kids about her age walking along the sidewalk. She liked the over-size ten gallon hats, neon jeans, cowboy boots and electro-plaid Smart shirts. There were some geeks too, just like her, passing by in the neighbouring Slider lane dressed in the latest tech clothing. She'd blend in just fine.

Chapter Five
HOPKINS

The Grooverider navigated the wide expanse of Market Street, waiting midway for an old-fashioned cable car to pass on its metal tracks. Its red and gold car was crammed full of tourists, the conductor furiously ringing the bell at a Slider rider who was in the way.

Nat stared through the window, soaking up the city vibe. It was so different to London where the Victorian fashion of long skirts, top hats and Penny Farthing bicycles was everywhere. And to Hong Kong where most people moved around town on sleek Sliders, wearing neon designer gear.

Things were more casual here, more laid back. People were walking slowly, taking their time. Their robots were perched on their shoulders, hats and backpacks. Most had the popular Soyto robot range, "Super-Cute, Fresh and Furry", with fully-waterproof, self-cleaning hair and everlasting-velvet ear-linings. She spotted skunks, racoons, wolves, moose and dinosaurs. Most of them were the latest models, only a few months old at the most. She couldn't imagine what it was like to trade in your old robot for a new one. Fizz had been with her since the day she was born.

The Grooverider started to climb up a steep hill.

"It's rather like the Peak, isn't it?" said Aunt Vera, as they crested the top and passed a towering cathedral. Trust her aunt to mention the Peak. She'd always wanted to live up there, back in Hong Kong, where the mansions of the billionaires looked down on the rest of the city.

The Grooverider moved along the top of the hill where huge, stately apartment blocks lined the street. In between the buildings Nat glimpsed the city and Bay stretching out below. They reached the other side and passed through a set of tall, iron gates into a sweeping driveway, pulling up in front of The Mark Hopkins Hotel. A man in a blue and gold uniform came running out and opened the Grooverider door.

"Welcome to The Mark," he said, popping his head inside and saluting Aunt Vera. "Will you be checking in or are you here to dine, ma'am?"

"Checking in. We are the Walkers," she replied, putting heavy emphasis on the family name like they were some kind of royalty.

INDIGO ISLAND

The doorman's white-gloved hand shot out to take her bony hand. "Mrs Walker, ma'am, we are delighted to have you all here. It is an honour."

Nat saw her aunt's "cat that got the cream" smile as she stepped out of the Grooverider.

"Hey, sleepyhead," she said to Henry. "We're here. Your mum has booked us into the swankiest hotel. It looks like The Peninsula and she's acting like the queen."

She pulled NutNut out from under Henry's head. The squashed squirrel let out a sigh of relief and set about using its paws to fluff up its fur. Henry opened his eyes. They were still ringed with goggle shadow.

"I just want to sleep," he moaned, curling up on the seat.

"Hey little fella, let me give you a hand out," said the doorman, sticking his cheery face back inside.

Nat waited for him to coax Henry out of the Grooverider. She stepped out just as a group of uniformed staff came stampeding out of the hotel, towards them.

"Welcome to The Mark, Mrs Walker. I am Sergio, the hotel manager. I trust you've had a great journey here. The Bullion Suite is ready and waiting for you, " said a tall man in a blue suit.

Her aunt let out a tinkling, girly laugh. "Thank you. I must say we are a little fatigued from our travels."

Nat wondered what had happened to her aunt's accent. She was suddenly sounding like a very posh lady from an old-fashioned movie where they wore corsets and bonnets.

"Then let us get you unloaded and I will personally show you to your suite." He turned to Nat. "Welcome, Miss."

"May I present Natalie Walker, my niece."

Nat could see the cogs in his brain begin to click and spin. A big, wide, brilliant-white smile spread across his face. "It is an honour to meet you, Miss Walker. Your grandfather was a patron of ours for many years."

The secret was out. All eyes turned to her, the SPIN orphan heiress. She could feel her cheeks burn with embarrassment. Fizz leaned his snout close to her ear. *"Have an open face, but conceal your thoughts,"* he whispered. She forced herself to look up from the cobblestones and smile at the crowd.

"Ah yes, Mr Drew. Nat's grandfather was such a wonderful man. We are here on family business actually, concerning his estate. I understand his old residence is not far from here," said Aunt Vera, her voice loud enough for anyone on the street to hear what she had to say.

So much for being below the radar. They were staying in one of the fanciest hotels, and now she was busy telling everyone about their business.

"Indeed. It's across on Russian Hill. The house was such a generous donation to the Asian Art Museum, it gets thousands of visitors a year. Any time you need to go there the hotel's Overrider is at your disposal."

Aunt Vera sniffed. "The house is a generous *loan* to the museum."

There was an awkward silence. The word "loan" hung in the air with a big question mark after it. A cloud briefly passed across Sergio's face. Nat was now officially squirming.

"The Bullion Suite butler, Hopkins, will be at your disposal to take care of your every need."

Aunt Vera squealed with delight.

"*Your temporary guardian is being most out of character,*" whispered Fizz, leaning his snout close in to Nat's ear.

"My own butler? Oh Sergio, you are too much."

A man with black, slicked-back hair and a smooth, movie-star face moved out of the middle of the group of waiting staff. Aunt Vera's face lit up. She clapped her hands together. As the butler came towards her the sound of horse's hooves echoed across the cobblestones.

"Hopkins at your service, Mrs Walker," he said, with a bow.

"Oh goodness!" said Aunt Vera, her hand flying to her throat.

Nat gulped. The top half of Hopkins' body was an android man. From the waist down it looked like he was wearing a pair of brown, hairy trousers, but they were long, robotic horse legs that ended in a pair of red glossy hooves.

"Ooo, it's Mr Tumnus!" said Henry.

"Hopkins is the very latest technological advancement, a hybrid robot made especially for the hospitality industry. The android upper can serve and carry out orders to the highest standard of service, and the lower racehorse legs can carry out the orders at top speed. It arrived from China today, already uploaded with our hotel practices, code of conduct and San Francisco knowledge bank. We thought it most fitting that you are its first clients," said Sergio, with a bow.

"Well, um thank you," said Aunt Vera.

"Never trust an android hybrid," whispered Fizz.

Chapter Six
THE BULLION SUITE

Nat hadn't stayed in many hotels in her life. She'd always slept in her cabin on board the *Junko*, unless she and Jamuka had taken a trip inland, and that was rare. They both liked to be near or on the water. The hotels that they'd stayed in had been plain and functional, the kind that business travellers used.

The Mark Hopkins was like some sort of palace. It had a huge marble entrance with red carpets. A massive chandelier, dripping with crystals, hung from the ceiling. The walls were lined with oil paintings of life in early San Francisco. Tall, potted palms divided clusters of deep, velvet sofas. A few guests were seated, drinking cocktails. Most of them were wearing the Goldrush fashion.

Sergio bypassed the main reception desk and whisked them straight into a glass elevator.

"The Bullion Suite has its own elevator," he said, as it moved off upwards at lightning speed.

Hopkins must have galloped up the stairs because

when the doors opened it was standing waiting.

"*You see. It over-performs,*" whispered Fizz.

"You're just jealous," said Nat.

Fizz huffed out a puff of smoke. "*No I am not. I have read the reviews and it is a conflicted robot – android brain and half-body designed to be like a human, but the horse legs need a different programming variance. They haven't worked out how to do it. Most likely they never will. I repeat, never trust an android hybrid.*"

"But you're a dragon with a human kind of brain."

He snorted. "*That's different. My brain is optimised to be a dragon. I am a dragon, not a half android like Hopkins.*"

She patted his wing. "I get you." She was too tired for robot logic right now.

"May I present The Bullion Suite," said Sergio, waving his hand like a magic wand.

Aunt Vera removed her Shan-xi coat and tossed it to Hopkins. "I think this will do nicely. A real home from home."

"This is way better than our—"

Henry didn't get to finish his sentence because Aunt Vera's hand shot out and covered his mouth. "Enough, Henry. Stay with Nat while I speak with Sergio."

She turned, linked arms with Sergio and moved him off into a cavernous sitting room with panoramic views of the city.

"May I show you to your rooms?" said Hopkins.

"We can find them ourselves," snapped Fizz, before Nat had a chance to reply.

She turned down the hallway that led from the sitting room, wanting to get out of earshot. "That's not like you. It was really rude," she said.

"Hopkins doesn't have a robot trust certificate. Its hybrid make isn't registered."

"I'm hungry," said Henry, catching them up.

"Go and ask Hopkins for whatever you want," said Nat.

"Anything?"

"Yes, anything. He says he can get anything, so give it a go."

Henry grinned and ran back, while she and Fizz started their own tour of the suite. No wonder it was called The Bullion Suite – all of the furniture was upholstered in shiny gold fabric, the curtains were gold, and the ceilings were mirrored so that everything was reflected in a golden light.

They were about to enter the next room when the door opened. Sergio appeared with Aunt Vera.

"Ah Natalie. No need for you to come in. This is the master bedroom so naturally I'll be residing in here."

She caught a glimpse of a gold four-poster bed decorated with flying swans. Her aunt was welcome to it.

"Henry can go in the room next to me, and I'm thinking you might want your own space so why not take the bedroom at the end, next to the elevator?"

Sergio cleared his throat. "Ah, that's the room most guests use for their staff, Mrs Walker. Perhaps Miss Walker might prefer the bedroom next to yours, and we can set up the luxe, King-Royale sofa-bed in the sitting room for your son."

Aunt Vera pursed her lips into a thin smile.

"Henry needs to be near me, and I don't want our sitting room turned into a bedsit. Natalie will be perfectly all right in the other room. She's used to a small cabin on her boat."

Secretly, Nat was delighted. Anything to be as far away from her aunt as possible. And being next to the elevator meant she could come and go without being easily detected.

She hurried off down the hallway to a narrow door with a brass plaque on it, which read "*Staff Room*".

She turned the knob and headed inside.

"*How very Cinderella,*" said Fizz.

There was enough room for a narrow, single bed. A small wardrobe and desk were built into the wall. The brown veneer was chipped off in places and she could see patches of glue where someone had tried to stick it back together. A threadbare, brown carpet covered the floor. There were a few stains on it and a burnt area in the shape of an iron. The window at the end looked out on to the hotel's main air-conditioning unit.

"The thing is, Fizz, I don't plan on spending much time in here at all. We've got a sword to find, and as soon as the *Junko* arrives, we're moving straight back on to it with Ah Ping. And, if we're lucky, we can leave Aunt Vera here."

Fizz's eyes flashed purple. "*A good, logical assessment of the situation. I like your plan.*"

"Hey Nat, look at this!"

Henry appeared in the doorway holding the tallest glass of strawberry, orange and chocolate ice cream that she'd ever seen.

"It's called a Knickerbocker Glory!" he said, grinning. "Want one?"

"Looks *ding*, but no thanks."

Aunt Vera's stilettos came clicking along the hallway.

"Ah, Henry, there you are!" she called.

Henry looked from his glass to Nat. "She'll never let me eat this," he said, eyes wide with panic.

Nat pointed to the bathroom. Henry ran inside and locked the door.

"Natalie. I thought I just saw Henry," said Aunt Vera, walking in.

"He needed the loo," said Nat.

"Oh, right. You've found your room then. It's quite … charming isn't it?"

Nat let out a huge yawn and stretched her arms wide.

"It's *ku*. I really need to rest after the long journey, if you don't mind?"

Her aunt reached out and patted her on the shoulder, as if she was petting a dog. "Of course. You must be tired. Sergio has invited us for lunch down in the restaurant, but I will make my excuses for you, and Henry too, since you can look after him."

Before Nat could reply Aunt Vera turned and left.

"Henry, you can come out now," called Nat. "Your mum's gone so let's get our plan sorted."

Chapter Seven
SCORTA

Zixin sat on the steps of the cathedral. For once he was glad to have Scorta with him as a cold, clammy fog had come creeping in from the ocean and blanketed the city. It was like sitting next to a furry radiator.

They'd been waiting for over half an hour. He was tired from the day, but even more so from jet lag. His eyelids grew heavy. If only he could just lie down, he'd be asleep in a second. His legs ached from walking up and down hills in his Slider boots.

His grandad had forbidden him to hire a Slider since he had Scorta. But there was no way he would ever get on the guinea-lion and ride it around the city. It was bad enough just walking next to it.

He looked up California Street to where The Mark Hopkins Hotel was hiding behind the veil of fog. Nat was lucky. She'd be inside in her luxury suite right now. It'd no doubt be warm and she could order up anything she wanted. His stomach grumbled. He hadn't eaten all day and he couldn't do anything about it until they'd met up with the weird androbot.

He shuddered. Androids were bad enough, but the weirdo man/horse bot was off-the-charts freaky. It'd been delivered by courier from his grandad's warehouse. He'd had to help unwrap it and lift it up on to the consulting room couch. Then he and Hong had unscrewed the top of its head and spent hours fiddling with tricky nano tools inside its bot brain, while his grandad sat perched on its body giving the orders.

Once activated, it had risen from the couch like Frankenstein's monster and introduced itself as "Hopkins". It was going to be a spy butler. A call was made to a friend of Hong's who was the robot resources manager at the hotel. Hong had dropped Hopkins off at the staff entrance, along with the suitcase full of dollars that had secured his swift appointment to "Butler of the Bullion Suite".

The clippety-clop of horse hooves came sounding through the fog. Hopkins appeared at a fast trot. "*Greetings,*" it said, with its smarmy smile.

Zixin stood up. He couldn't look it in the eye so he focused on Scorta's guinea pig face instead. Even that was preferable to the androbot.

"*Pass me the file,*" squeaked Scorta.

INDIGO ISLAND

The androbot's eyes flashed ice-blue as it connected direct to Scorta and passed the file. Zixin yawned. *"Transfer complete,"* it said.

"Has anyone talked about a sword?" said Zixin.

Hopkins paused, tracking through the file.

"No but I have not been privy to all conversations. The dragon robot does not trust me and has banned me from Natalie Walker's room."

"Drat that dragon!" said his grandad, inside his ear. *"I must return to the suite before Mrs Walker finishes her lunch with the hotel manager. They were on the dessert course when I left."*

"Tell him to go, and you get back here fast, my boy," said his grandad in his ear.

"Go. We'll meet you here tomorrow morning at seven."

Hopkins saluted and galloped off back up California Street. Shrieks and screams came echoing out of the fog as he sped past a group of tourists on the cable car.

"Hop on and let's get going," squeaked Scorta.

"I'd rather eat pieces of glass than get on you."

The guinea-lion scowled. *"Suit yourself. Not good enough for you, are we?"*

"You're a freak."

He knew he shouldn't even go there, but he was

tired, cold and hungry. The nip was fast and furious. He felt the titanium teeth pierce the skin of his cheek.

"Get on!" growled Scorta.

Zixin was too tired and hungry to argue. He swung his leg over its back, put his head low and gripped on to the mane. Scorta took off at a run, hurtling down Nob Hill like a bullet, straight into Chinatown.

They came flying through Hong's door into the consulting room, where Scorta bucked Zixin off. He hit the hard tile floor, knocking the wind out of himself.

His grandad flapped down from his perch and landed on Zixin's chest. He leaned over so that his big, bald head was right in Zixin's face.

"My boy. The rules from now on. You behave. No talk back, no robot bashing, just follow orders and you'll see your snake again. Got it?"

His grandad's breath was fetid and fishy. Zixin nodded. He'd agree to anything right now. "And remember … I can always make a hybrid out of you."

Those words were so chilling that Zixin froze. It was clear that the only way forward was to obey, to do as he was told, no matter what his grandad asked him to do.

Chapter Eight
SLIDERS 'R' US

Dry land didn't rock or sway in the night like the *Junko*. Nat tossed and turned in her bed, listening to the air conditioning unit outside rumbling like a wok-oil-fuelled truck. She'd been stuck in this stuffy room since they'd arrived because Henry had been so jet-lagged that he'd fallen asleep on her bed, and she didn't want to leave him on his own. She'd tried hanging out in the sitting room but Hopkins would stand at the door asking her every five minutes if she required anything. Fizz kept telling her he didn't trust it, and kept blasting out long plumes of white smoke from his snout if it got too close.

"What time is it?"

Fizz's eyes snapped open. Two bright green spotlights cut through the darkness like a pair of lasers.

"Five thirty am, Pacific time," he said, from where he was perched on the door handle.

He'd insisted on being on guard all night, an ear pressed against the door so that he could keep track of Hopkins. Nat switched on the bedside light and swung her legs off the bed. She needed to escape and start her search for the sword.

She pulled on her Slider jacket, leggings and boots. "*Zoula!* The plan begins."

They opened the bedroom door as quietly as possible, leaving a gap just big enough for Fizz to poke his snout out.

"*Hopkins is standing in front of the elevator in guard mode,*" he said, reporting back.

"Tell it we need something. Something it has to go and get," she whispered.

Fizz's eyes flashed as he processed options and solutions.

"*The 24/7 US Pharmacy on the Embarcadero has the Bigtastic hair spray that I'd like to use the next time you ask me to style your hair. It has a stronger hold than the one I used, so it'll last all day. I could relay that information to Hopkins and insist that you require immediate delivery.*"

She nodded. "Good thinking, go do it."

He was about to fly out through the open crack but stopped and turned back to her.

"*I lie for you out of love,*" he said, his eyes glowing purple.

She stood staring at him, letting the words sink in. For the first time ever he'd gone beyond his robot logic to make an emotional decision.

"I love you too," she said.

He spread his wings and flew out into the hallway. She didn't dare peep out to see how he did it – Hopkins might see her. So she waited, ear pressed against the door. It was hard to hear though because the air conditioning unit outside the window upped its rumbling as hotel staff and guests began their day.

A snout appeared through the crack.

"The androbot is gone. It didn't want to leave its post but I overrode its authority and dispatched it."

She stepped out into the hallway. "Let's do it." she said, heading into the elevator.

They sneaked out of the side entrance, avoiding the doorman, on to a steep street. Nat shivered in the early morning fog. It was as cold and damp here as it had been in London. Seagulls flew squawking overhead, and the drone of early morning traffic filtered up from the streets below.

"Follow me. The GrooveCab I booked is waiting for us at Clay and Mason," said Fizz, flying across the road.

Nat crossed quickly, then started jogging after him

to keep warm. They reached the other side of the hill and descended to the GrooveCab waiting on a street corner. You couldn't miss it since it was bright yellow and covered in flashing musical notes.

"*Walker, yeah?*" said the raccoon-robot driver through its lowered window.

"*Affirmative,*" said Fizz.

The automatic door popped open and Nat hopped into the warmth. A saxophone was accompanying a man belting out "*I'm blue about you baby*" through a pair of worn-out, crackly speakers.

They raced down to the bottom of the hill and turned right into a wide avenue. The racoon drove them a few blocks to where a neon green "Sliders'R'Us" sign was flashing through the veil of fog. It pulled up outside just as the singer finished up "*Baby, baby, baby, you got me blue!*"

She jumped out, leaving Fizz to pay the bill. She never wanted to get in a GrooveCab again. Her ears were ringing and now she was feeling blue too.

A hip Slider boy avatar suddenly appeared right in front of her. "*Welcome, Natalie Walker! We've got your booking for the basic Slide'n'Glide package. Can I interest you in an upgrade to our wider Slider range?*"

Rat's tails! She realised that she'd forgotten to remove the identity micro dot that she'd been issued with at immigration. It was part of the "California Tourist" promotion that they gave to visitors. She reached into her jacket pocket, pulled out the SmartCard ID, hooked a nail under the stick-on micro dot in the top corner of her photograph, and flicked it off into the nearby garbage bin.

"No thanks, just the basic package we ordered."

The electric-blue boy gave the garbage can a thumbs-up. "Great! Follow me and we'll get you sorted."

He hovered, waiting for the microdot to start moving. She left him waiting and headed up the steps, through the sliding doors and into a room filled with rack after rack of multi-coloured Sliders.

Chapter Nine
POPKO AND PANCAKES

The Slider was twice as wide as the one Nat normally rode. It was heavier too, and slow as a slug. Worse still the board was covered in swirly, flowery patterns and had a big red heart in the middle. The words *"Flower Power"* were written in curly pink writing across the top. She was too young to be able to hire anything faster, and unable to get anything without the "Summer Of Love" theme scrawled all over it.

Nat pulled out into the Slider lane and joined the steady flow, headed out towards the Golden Gate Bridge. Everyone was moving at cruising speed. Cowboys and cowgirls were tipping their ten gallon hats to each other, exchanging "howdy" greetings as they sipped coffee from takeaway mugs. Geeks in shiny Slider suits were on calls, talking loudly about the latest tech news. No one seemed to be focused on the actual art of riding a Slider, or in a hurry to get to where they were headed.

Nat was used to London and Hong Kong where

no-one cruised. They raced and jostled.

"They're moving like tortoises! It'll take us all day to get to grandfather's house," she groaned. "Isn't there another way we can go?"

"*There are routes along parallel streets but they are without Slider lanes. In a foreign country with customs that we have yet to fully comprehend I have calculated it is safer to travel on main routes...*"

Nat leaned hard left. The Slider followed her movement and they swerved, narrowly missing a cowboy on a double-wide board.

"Hey, little lady!" he shouted, spilling coffee down his checked shirt.

She darted into a side street, lined with parked high-end Overriders and Grooveriders.

"*You're on the wrong side of the road!*" shouted Fizz, his snout flashing like a red police siren.

Tiger's teeth! An old pickup truck was racing headlong towards them. The truck driver honked his horn. She leaned hard right, whipping them over to the other side of the road, just in time. They missed each other by the width of a noodle.

"That was a bit close," she said, easing up on her speed.

"*That was a rash move and corresponds directly*

to your risk-taking tendencies, which have increased sharply since you entered your teenage years due to an imbalance between your prefrontal cortex and nucleus accumbent," said Fizz.

"Don't give me a lecture now. I couldn't stand the snail's pace. Look, this is much better!"

She'd turned into a long, quiet road lined with trees and glossy, white, wooden apartment buildings. A couple of young women were jogging along the sidewalk dressed in the latest UrbRun suits, with neon-lit active seams that heated and cooled the runners' bodies to maintain optimum muscle performance. She smiled. If Wen was with her she'd be saying how *ding* and on-trend they were because one of the suits was printed with pink flamingo bird feathers, and the other with orange goldfish scales.

"Teenagers require an increased intake of calories to facilitate their development, so I have located a PPJ café for breakfast. It is located seven blocks from here," said Fizz.

"What's PPJ?"

"Popko, Pancake and Juice."

Popko? Just the name of her favourite juice made her tastebuds tingle.

"Didn't know they did pancakes too."

"Only in the United States of America."

Her stomach growled, her mouth began watering.

"Show me the way!" she said, pushing the handlebars forward to pick up speed.

A stars and stripes flag flew over the entrance to PPJ's. She jumped down off her Slider and found a slot for it in a rack outside. A large sign hung over the glass entrance doors, "*100% genuinely authentic live humans waiting on you in here.*"

She headed into the busy cafe.

"Hey there. How are you doing today? I like your jacket. That's one cool, kick-ass scene you're playing on it," said a waiter, handing her a SmartSheet menu and taking her over to a table next to the window.

She took a seat. Fizz flew off her shoulder to perch on the table, so that they could both scan the menu, while the waiter carried on talking at a million miles an hour.

"We've got a triple stack of blueberry maple pancakes on special, cream on the side. The Popko juice of the day is mango and strawberry with a bubble twist of fifty percent Peruvian origin chocolate. Would you like a few minutes or are you ready to POP your order in now?"

She couldn't wait a few more minutes. The sweet

smell of fresh, warm pancakes was driving her bonkers.

"I'll have the special pancakes and juice, thanks."

The waiter gave her a fifty kilowatt smile. "Great! I'll get right to it. Awesome dragon by the way." Before she could reply, he'd hurried off towards the kitchen.

Nat looked around the cafe. Nearly all the tables were full. People and robots were chatting loudly. She wondered if her mum had ever been in here when she was growing up. She pictured her sitting at the same table, reading her ancient history books, or hanging out with a friend.

Her mum had been an only child, just like her, but she was born before people had robots. She wouldn't have had a buddy like Fizz to hang out with all the time. All you had back then was some kind of smart phone, like a block that you put in your pocket, or a fold-out laptop that you had to cart around in a backpack.

She put her hand out and stroked Fizz's scaly head. He was her trusted friend, with his glittering mesh of feather-light scales, micro-chips, nano sensors and robotic limbs. They shared the same birthday because her dad had designed and built him to activate the moment she was born.

Being fourteen years old in the robot world meant he was classed as vintage, but since his latest upgrade he could fly as fast as an arrow, blow long-plume smoke and flames, and talk like a human. His silver talons were so strong that he could hang upside down like a bat, and stay gripped on to a sail rope in a force ten gale. Nat couldn't imagine life without him.

The waiter arrived with her order. The triple stack of pancakes rose up in a fluffy tower. They gleamed with a thick sheen of maple syrup. Fizz stuck his snout into the bowl of whipped cream.

"What are you doing?"

"*It is ninety-five percent dairy, five percent icing sugar,*" he said, lifting his head. "*I wanted to ascertain how they created the perfectly formed, whipped structure.*"

She wiped the cream off him with her napkin.

"Please don't do the same to the pancakes."

She speared the pancakes with her fork, and let the knife slip down through the stack. The moment the pancakes touched her lips the warm blueberry and maple flavours exploded into her mouth. She took another bite, then another, followed by a slurp of Popko juice.

"*Zoinks!* That's *ding* and delicious!" she said,

licking her lips.

"Sugar fuel burns bright."

She carried on, slurping the juice and munching the pancakes. When she was only a third of the way through the stack she stopped, fork poised at her open mouth. Out of the corner of her eye she spotted a horse and rider trotting along the street in the Slider lane. As it got closer though she saw it wasn't a horse at all, it was a lion with a shaggy mane. She must be seeing things. She rubbed her eyes, but sure enough it really was a giant lion, but it had the face of a guinea pig! She gasped.

"Fizz…"

But the words escaped her because the rider looked up. She froze. Zixin's dark, piercing eyes met hers. His mouth opened, his snake tongue flicked out. He started shouting something at the lion-pig. It took off at a gallop up the street.

Nat leapt up from the table and sprinted towards the door. The other diners turned to stare. Fizz came swooping after her.

"We have to pay!" he shouted.

She wasn't listening. She burst on to the sidewalk, jumped onboard her Slider and went chasing after her mortal enemy.

Chapter Ten
HONEY

Scorta didn't stop until it reached Hong's. Zixin slid off the lion's back and caught his breath. It'd been a wild ride. He'd need a saddle if he was going to have to get around the city at that speed.

At the early morning meeting at the cathedral steps Hopkins had reported that it had been duped into leaving the hotel by Nat's dragon and when it had returned, she was gone. After that they'd been on a mission to find her. She and Fizz were in ghost mode. Zixin had tried to hack into their comms using every trick he knew, but they'd cloaked their traffic. That dragon was smart.

Eventually, he'd set up a tracer on any financial transactions she made. When Nat had hired the Slider, Scorta received an alert. They'd raced over to the Slider store. Zixin tried to spin a story that he was a friend of Nat's, that they were on holiday together from London, and that she'd got up and gone out before him, so now he needed the tracer ID on her

Slider to find her.

The man refused to give it him. So Scorta transferred six months' salary into the man's account.

"You must really like her," he'd said, handing over the ID.

Even so, seeing Nat in the cafe had caught Zixin by surprise because he was tracking her Slider, which she'd parked around the block. For a split second he hadn't recognised her choppy blue hair and silver lashes. It was the scaly top of Fizz's head that gave her away. And just as he'd realised that, she'd looked up and stared right at him. Those green eyes of hers had said it all:

Who are you?

Zixin?

I hate you!

It had been brilliant to have a real friend. But now they were enemies instead.

"Why did you come back you fools! You are chasing the girl, she is not chasing you!" screamed his grandad. He came flapping through from the consulting room and slapped Zixin across the face with his wing. "Where's the girl?"

"*She followed us up Nob Hill before we lost her.*

She's now headed over to Russian Hill towards the museum," reported Scorta.

"Then what are you waiting for? Get over there NOW!"

Zixin didn't reply. He walked out of the door and into the heaving mass of city folk, all doing normal things like shopping and sightseeing. They weren't chasing after someone, hoping they'd find some mythical sword, which would animate a robot army to conquer the world. They hadn't had the only thing they loved in the world stolen from them, held hostage, until they'd completed some crazy life-and-death task.

He ignored his grandad's rant into his ear about waiting for Scorta, and took off at a run, dodging in and around the crowds. He wasn't sure where he was going, he just wanted to put some distance between him and the terrible things that now ruled his life.

He reached Columbus Street and carried on running towards the waterfront. His grandad was now screaming in his ear that he needed to get up Russian Hill and get to work again. No way. He spotted a natural food store and ran inside.

"Do you have any runny honey?" he asked the woman at the counter.

"Yeah, we've got acacia, honeysuckle, and I think we might have a jar left of that awesome Hawaiian Kiawe tree blossom."

"Which is the thickest, but still runs fast off a spoon?"

"Neat question! I don't get asked that every day. I'd say the acacia 'cos it comes in a squeeze tube with a pointy cap."

"What are doing buying honey you idiot?" screamed his grandad, so loud that Zixin had to close his eyes, squeezing them tight shut to try to block out the pain.

"You okay?" The woman put her hand on his arm. "Stay there, I'll get it for you."

Zixin handed over $10 and ran out of the store.

"Hey, don't you want your change?" she shouted after him.

He could tell Scorta had found him because people were screaming, turning to stare, ordering their robots to capture a photo of it.

"*Can't escape us,*" squeaked the guinea pig, reaching out and nipping him on the hand.

Zixin snatched his hand away. A bead of blood was already forming on the skin.

"I need the loo," he said, heading into a bright, tile-fronted cafe.

INDIGO ISLAND

He made his way through the busy tables of coffee drinkers towards the back. Once inside the men's toilet, he locked the door, ripped the top off the honey, cocked his head to one side, and squirted it into his ear.

Chapter Eleven
THE GOAT

Nat jumped off her Slider, propped it against the stone column and rapped the brass knocker on the massive entrance doors. She could hear the sound echoing inside. Her grandfather's house was way bigger than how it looked in the Asian Art Museum's guide.

"We may have to wait a further hour until the official opening time," said Fizz, from his perch on her shoulder.

She didn't want to wait. She wanted to get inside and get hunting for the sword right away. Seeing that rotten, snake-tongued boy in the street on that monstrous lion-pig robot had made her blood boil. If she'd had her own Slider with her, and not the stupid flower-power slug, she'd have caught up with him, used a flying kick and booted him off his robot, knocking him unconscious to the ground.

Then she'd have locked him up in The Bullion Suite, with the weird androbot Hopkins guarding him, until she'd found the Gan Jiang sword and escaped the city.

Instead he'd got away, but it wouldn't be long before he came back.

She rapped the knocker again, harder so that it banged on the door like a sledgehammer. There was the sound of clomping boots. The bolts drew back, the door opened, and a man in a black and gold peaked cap stuck his head out.

"You woke me up! Now scram, we don't open for another hour."

"I'm Natalie Walker, daughter of Catherine Walker, granddaughter of Walter Drew, and I need to come in, please," she said.

The man yawned.

"And I'm the president of the United States of America," he said, withdrawing his head.

Fizz blasted out a stream of flames that licked around the side of the door before it shut.

"*That will wake the president up*," said Fizz.

There was a roar of fury and the door flew open. The guard reappeared. A wisp of smoke was curling off the peak of his cap. He was reaching for the gun in his holster when a miniature silver goat robot came charging across the marble behind him, hooves clipping the marble floor. It lowered its head, and butted him in the bottom with its horns, tossing him up into the air.

"Oof!" said the guard, landing in a heap on the floor.

"Greetings, Natalie. I have been waiting for you," said the goat, in a gruff voice. *"I'm Mister Drew's personal goat, and you will follow me."*

Nat had never seen a robot like this one before. Her grandfather's goat was made of leaf-patterned sheets of silver. Its horns were glossy and black. Its eyes were glistening pools of liquid silver, in the middle of which were jewel-like aquamarine pupils.

"This way, please," it said, turning on its hooves and trotting towards a large sweeping staircase.

"I like this robot," whispered Fizz. *"It's small, perfectly formed, fully certified from the last century, and it knows how to straight-talk and get things done. Did you see the way it achieved such high and long trajectory when it butted the guard? I'm going to learn from it,"* whispered Fizz.

So this was the house where her mum had grown up. As she climbed the staircase, it hit her. This was now hers. She'd inherited this massive mansion with its silk-lined walls, sweeping staircase and endless rooms – they all belonged to her.

"*Come on! Keep moving, Natalie,*" shouted the goat.

She carried on climbing until she reached Fizz and the goat, standing side by side on the top step. She'd been so mesmerised that she hadn't even realised that her dragon had left her shoulder. Now they were together she could see how similar the two robots were. One might be a dragon and the other a goat, but the way they'd been designed with their shimmering metal bodies and the way they were looking at her could only mean one thing…

"Did my dad make you?" she said to the goat.

The goat stamped one of its front hooves. "*Sure did. He was a fine man, your dad. Made me for Mister Drew. I'm a one-off, ass-kicking dude-goat.*"

Fizz blew out a long plume of white smoke. "*He made me, too. Hello, my brother.*"

The goat high-fived Fizz's wing with his hoof.

"*Hey bro', good to make your acquaintance.*"

"*Likewise, dear fellow,*" said Fizz, putting on his best knights-of-the-realm English accent.

The goat turned back to Nat. "*I served your grandfather well for many years. I was automatically deactivated the day he died, but he programmed me to reactivate for you, when the time came."*

"How did you know it was me?" she said.

"I am a trained DNA sniffer."

She'd never heard of one. She looked at Fizz. He shrugged.

"And what do you mean *when the time came*?"

The goat let out a long, low bleat like it'd been saving up a sigh for all the years it'd been an exhibit on her grandfather's desk.

"Follow me," said the goat, trotting off down a long corridor hung with paintings of monks.

She could hear Fizz chatting to the goat as he flew. She couldn't make out what he was saying but she guessed he'd have at least a million questions for his newly discovered brother. All she wanted to know was what *"when the time came"* meant. The sigh, the words, sounded like a whole lot of bad news.

The goat stopped outside a door marked *"No Access Permitted"* and head-butted it open. They came out into another corridor, which was lined with offices. They were all empty, except for one, which was occupied by a couple of androids who were quietly stuffing traditional paper envelopes with thick, gold-edged invitations.

At the end of the hallway they climbed another

flight of stairs, and then another, which led up to a secure metal door that read "*Roof Access: Authorised Personnel Only*". The goat used its horns to lift up a small side panel at floor level, and put its front left hoof inside. The metal door slid open.

"*Access granted,*" said an automated voice.

Thick fog came gusting into the hallway.

"*Let's do this,*" said the goat, trotting out on to a flat roof.

Nat stepped out and the door slid shut behind her. It was like standing on a football pitch – a slippy one, as the black roof tar was coated in misting moisture. In the middle stood a satellite dish that was so big it could probably communicate with aliens.

The goat was standing moving its head from left to right, right to left.

"So, why are we here?" she asked, zipping her jacket up against the cold.

Chapter Twelve
HEIRESS

He might now be deaf in his left ear since it was flooded with honey and plugged with loo roll, but Zixin didn't care. He couldn't hear his grandad any more because the nano-implant couldn't work properly in all the goop. It had stopped transmitting his location, too, so he had bought himself some time. Not that it would stop Scorta from hunting him down. That evil guinea pig head would probably already be sniffing out his trail with its Pherowiff sensors.

He ran fast, using side streets, all the way down to Fisherman's Wharf. He spotted a large group of school kids up ahead who were about his age. He caught up with them and hid himself in the middle of their huddle to think about his next move.

"Dude, what's with the snake tongue?"

Zixin turned to find a boy in an LA Dodgers baseball cap standing next to him. Both he and his chipmunk robot were staring at him. He quickly shut his mouth. He had a bad habit of flicking his tongue out when he was deep in thought. Instead of getting salty with the boy, he ducked out of the group.

In front of him stood a ramshackle wooden pier lined with gift shops. He needed a disguise, fast. He hurried past shops selling souvenirs – t-shirts, Slider shorts, coffee mugs and key rings, all with some type of "San Francisco" stamp on them. That would be too obvious. It was all right to wear that kind of gear down here near the water, but back downtown those threads would make him a total standout.

At the end of the row he spotted an old-fashioned, hand-painted sign swinging from a metal bar: "*The Old Western Thrift Shop*". That sounded more up his street.

He headed in to find an old man dressed in a checked shirt and leather trousers, lying back in a rocking chair. He had his cowboy boots propped up on the counter, and his hat was tipped forward. He was snoring.

A small brown dog came whipping around the counter and started barking, making Zixin jump. He was used to robotic animals, but live ones were radically out of his comfort zone.

"Howdy," said the man, tipping back the brim of his ten-gallon hat.

Zixin nodded, skirted around the yapping dog, and headed over to a rack of shirts, blue jeans, and jackets marked *"Five bucks or less, take your pick"*. The clothes smelled like the reptile cage in London zoo. But the price was right and the smell would throw off the guinea-lion's Pherowiff sensors. He picked out a few things that looked as if they'd fit, and went into a changing room designed to look like a giant cactus.

He had very little money on him, just a few dollars that he'd found at Hong's. He wished now he'd picked up the change at the health food store when he'd bought the honey.

He emerged from the changing room in a pair of bootcut jeans, a red and blue checked shirt and a fringed brown suede coat. He couldn't afford replacement boots, but preferred his Slider ones anyway.

"Now ya look like a real cowboy," drawled the man, taking his cash and throwing in a battered ten gallon hat and red neckerchief for free.

With the last of his money he bought a pair of cheap, mirrored sunglasses in the shop next door then headed off towards Russian Hill and Nat's grandad's old pad.

Posh. It wasn't like one of the double-fronted, candy-coloured Victorian houses that he'd passed on his way up the steep, zig-zagging street. This was a real swag pad – a massive, three-storey, brick mansion covered in shiny green ivy. It reminded him of school, but this had been one family's house. His dad's flat in London would have fitted inside it a hundred times.

A black and gold "Asian Art Museum" flag was flying above the entrance doors, and a long queue of people waiting to get inside snaked along the side of the building.

He was about to cross over to join them when he caught sight of Scorta sitting next to a fire hydrant on the street corner. The creepy robot had a clear view of the front entrance, and was watching it intently with its beady guinea pig eyes. Was it waiting for him, for Nat, or both of them? Either way, he needed to slip past it.

Zixin backed off up the street to wait out of sight, until he spotted an old couple also dressed in cowboy gear getting out of a GrooveCab on the corner. He pulled up the collar on his jacket, tipped his hat forward to shade his face, and crossed over, giving himself a limp. He walked around the back of the cab so that it looked like he'd stepped out with them, and followed them closely, keeping just a step behind until they joined the museum line. The man pulled a SmartSheet out of his jacket pocket. When he unrolled it a map of the museum appeared, and he started to discuss what he wanted to see first with his wife.

"Excuse me, could you tell me what are the best things to see here?" said Zixin, in a fake American accent.

The lady turned towards him and smiled. "Well, you sure should see the group of Terracotta Warriors they've got here."

"Sounds awesome," said Zixin, keeping the conversation going until they were inside.

"Yeah. I've been reading that the man who used to live in this mansion brought them back with him all the way from China."

Her husband laughed. "You've got to have some serious money to even think of doing that kinda thing."

The woman lowered her voice as if she had some big secret to share. "They say his daughter married that billionaire games guy. She inherited this mansion, and then had all that games money too. She carried on the collectin' where her father left off. There's a sword collection of hers that I want to see. That was before she died in some kinda plane crash. Can you believe it? All that money and you still never know what's going to happen."

Zixin nodded. He could see Scorta scanning the line. It paused where he was standing. He bowed his head closer to the lady.

"That is tragic. Did she have any children?"

They were nearly at the doors.

"A daughter, so I understand. She's still a child, but she's got all this to herself."

Out of the corner of his eye he saw Scorta move its gaze further up the line.

"Wow, a rich heiress. I guess she must have an amazing life," he said, following them inside.

The man chuckled. "Hell yeah! I bet she does!"

Chapter Thirteen
DISCOVERY

A seagull perched on the corner of the roof was keeping a beady eye on Nat while she yawned and watched the robot goat and Fizz argue. The energy burst from the pancakes had worn off and she was as tired as a hundred year old dog.

They'd been up on the roof of the museum for a very long time. The goat was looking for something that her grandfather had hidden and it was taking forever to find the location, even for the whizz-brained robot.

The fog had finally lifted and the sun was now shining down from a bright blue sky. Nat wished she'd brought her sunglasses. Instead she squinted across the roof, checking out their progress. If she was lucky, the hidden secret would be Gan Jiang. She'd stuff it down inside her Slider outfit somehow and sneak out, back to the hotel.

"By my calculations, it's somewhere over there," said the goat, finally, pointing its horns to the corner of the roof, where the seagull was perched.

INDIGO ISLAND

The seagull wasn't at all happy to see them approaching. It adjusted its wings, opened its yellow beak and let out an ear-splitting screech. Fizz responded by swooping down from Nat's shoulder, spreading his wings and blasting a stream of smoke from his snout. The seagull took off. "*Ku.* Now where is this secret place?" said Nat.

"*Bottom row, five bricks along on the right,*" the goat said, pointing to a dull-red brick, just like the others.

She crouched down and traced over and around the brick with her fingers. It was cold and wet. It didn't move. She tried pressing it. Nothing.

"How does it work?"

"*I don't have that information,*" said the goat.

Rat's tails. Nat stared at the brick, lifted a Slider boot and gave it a kick. Solid, immovable brick wall met with the boot.

"Are you sure this is the right place?"

"*Sure is. Want me to give it a head butt?*"

The goat lowered its horns and scraped its hoof on the roof felt, ready to charge. She pictured it crashing straight through to thin air on the other side.

"No! Don't do that."

She stood up and leaned over the top of the wall.

Just bricks, stacked and cemented together. Looking down she could see the museum entrance, where a long line of visitors were queuing to get inside. Any bricks the goat knocked loose would land on some of them.

She was about to pull away when she became aware of something watching her from across the street. She froze. Two beady guinea pig eyes were staring up at her. Tiger's teeth! How could she have been so stupid? The pig-lion moved off its haunches. There was no sign of Zixin, though. Maybe he was already inside. She dropped back down behind the wall.

"That weird pig-lion's down there and it saw me! That means Zixin's here, too."

Fizz's eyes flashed red.

"*Are this pig-lion and Zixin a threat?*" said the goat, standing to attention with its small tail flicked upright.

"*They are foe who seek the sword of Gan Jiang,*" said Fizz.

The goat turned and bolted across the roof. "*I'll be at the door. No one's gonna get past me!*"

Nat knelt down and studied the brick closely. A second later there was a faint whirring sound inside the wall and the brick slid sideways, leaving a gap between the bricks. Of course! Eye retina recognition.

She reached inside the gap, into a cold, damp, hollow space. Her fingers touched upon metal. It must be the sword!

Chapter Fourteen
MacDUFF

Nat pulled out a metal canister with a screw top. Her heart sank. Unless Gan Jiang was tiny, like some kind of penknife, this wasn't it. She tried to twist the top but it was rusted shut.

"*May I assist you?*" said Fizz.

She held it out for him and he wrapped his talons around it. Rusty metal flakes came showering out as the top came off.

Fizz flew up on to her shoulder while she turned the canister upside down. A small roll of yellow paper, tied up with a piece of string, fell out into her palm. Her fingers fumbled with the tight knot.

It was an old SmartSheet with a photograph of her grandfather sitting at his oak desk. He was wearing a blue shirt, jacket and tie, and looked like a president about to give a speech to the nation. His grey hair was slicked back and he wore a pair of big, black-framed glasses.

She ran her fingers across the surface, activating

the film. The image flickered and her grandfather steepled his fingers together and leaned closer into camera.

"Hello, Natalie. We are meeting like this because both your mom and I will be gone by now, which is why my old goat will have led you to find this hidden message.

"As you know, there's a tradition in our family for collecting ancient artefacts. My house is full of them. It is now yours to look after, or you can leave that to those museum folk.

"Your mom grew up with all my stories about ancient stories and legends. Maybe she's told them to you too. Anyway there was one story she liked more than any other. She would insist that I tell her 'The myth of Gan Jiang and Mo Ye' every night before she went to sleep. That's what spurred her on to go to university to study the ancient world. I guess you could say I brought her up in an unconventional sort of way. You see, after my wife died so young I used to take her with me whenever I travelled on business, so she got to see many parts of the world.

"Anyway, I digress. Back to the swords. I thought they were just a good old bedtime story but she believed they were real.

"*Your mom became obsessed with finding them, and after all these years she and your dad say they have found Mo Ye I can't believe it, so I'm about to leave for England to go and see it for myself.*

"*However before I leave she's asked me to record this. She says it's in case anything happens. I don't know what she's worried about but I promised her I'd do this, so here goes…*

"*I got the sword story originally from your great-great uncle who used to be a prison guard on Alcatraz Island, way back when it was still a prison. Harold was his name, and when I was a boy he'd tell me stories about his time there.*

"*One of them was about a prisoner they called 'Mad MacDuff'. He was a hobo on the streets of San Francisco. They say he'd killed a man, and was found babbling next to the body in some made-up, crazy language.*

"*They locked him up on Alcatraz Island for his crime. MacDuff kept telling Harold that he'd gone mad because of a sword that he'd won off a Chinese railroad worker in a game of cards. He said it was called Gan Jiang, that it had magical properties and that it was so dangerous that he'd gone and hidden the sword for safety.*

INDIGO ISLAND

"One day MacDuff just went plain crazy in his cell, screaming that the sword was telling him to set it free. A thunderstorm came rolling in, churning up the waters in the Bay. Harold said he'd never seen anything like it before. Lightning forked over the prison, gargantuan waves crashed against its shores. He went to check on the prisoners. They were all there but one. The window bars in MacDuff's cell had been burned clean off by a lightning strike. He'd escaped.

"He didn't get far, though. His body washed up in Fisherman's Wharf the next morning, right outside Scoma's restaurant. The chef spotted him out of the kitchen window, floating face down.

"Harold was given the task of clearing his cell. He found a note tucked under MacDuff's mattress that said, 'If you read this then I'm gone for good. Gan Jiang needs Mo Ye. Look around this prison and you'll find out where I hid it. Sincerely, Ulysees MacDuff.'

"Harold started his search in the prison, but he found nothing. I searched as well when I was a boy. By then the prison had been closed, all the inmates had been transferred to other places, and it had been reopened as a tourist destination.

"It'd keep me from getting bored in the summer vacation. I'd take the ferry out there and spend whole days wandering the empty buildings, re-tracing MacDuff's daily routine. He worked over in the Model Industries building, exercised in the recreation yard, ate in the dining hall and did a stint in the library. I searched and searched, but found nothing.

"The good news is that I grew to love ancient mysteries and artefacts. That's why this house is full of the stuff.

"Your mom has also searched the whole of Alcatraz Island for the sword, but even with all her fire and gumption she's not found it. The secret still lies out there, somewhere.

"So there you have it, that's my story for you. Look after the house and especially my goat, who was fiercely loyal to me.

"My love to you Natalie."

He saluted to the camera. The paper turned blank. Nat stared at it for a long time, her face reflecting across its glossy surface. She knew her grandfather had never returned from that trip to England because he'd had a heart attack there and died. It must have happened only a few days after he'd recorded this film.

INDIGO ISLAND

"*Think we'd better scram if you're done,*" interrupted the goat, clattering across the roof towards them. "*There's reports of a security breach on the third floor!*"

Chapter Fifteen
A NARROW ESCAPE

Zixin had looked in every glass case, at every statue and every painting that there was in the museum. He'd moved from room to room, floor to floor, searching for clues, anything that might lead to the sword. The only thing that kept him going was Vesperetta. If he found the sword then he got her back, and that was all that mattered.

He'd been relying on the crowds around him to warn of Scorta's arrival. They were bound to freak out if the guinea-lion came wandering in. But neither clues nor Scorta had shown up.

He was in the last room on the top floor. Beyond it lay the end of the corridor, which was sealed off with a closed door saying *"No Public Access: Staff Only"*. The building was way bigger on the outside than the rooms he'd been able to get into. That meant only one thing, there had to be more rooms beyond that door.

Was Nat somewhere in there? What if she'd already found the sword and got away?

INDIGO ISLAND

The door had a RetScan next to it, so he had no chance of nipping in. If only he had Vesperetta with him, she'd have been able to slide underneath and check it out.

The answer to his problems came a few minutes later when a woman in a black suit headed to the door. The RetScan activated, the door opened. He glimpsed a long, brightly lit corridor beyond. She passed through, walking at speed.

He seized his chance and slipped through, unnoticed, behind her. He took off his hat and sunglasses, and ran his hands through his hair to smooth it into some sort of office-style.

The woman moved ahead quickly, her heels clicking on the black and white tiles. He followed in her wake, passing museum-administration offices with people busy at their desks.

They'd nearly reached the end of the corridor when the woman stopped to talk to someone through her nanodot earpiece. She began to turn on her heels. Zixin panicked and jumped into the closest office.

He found himself in a small, windowless room, which was divided into two cubicles. Each one was occupied by an android office worker, sitting at a screen loaded with accounting spreadsheets.

The one closest, a middle-aged male with grey hair, looked up at him. It was an out-of-the-box senior accountant android with classic, steel-rimmed glasses.

"May I assist you?" it said.

Hearing its voice made Zixin's skin crawl. "Um, I've been sent to check on the school-visit numbers," he mumbled.

The android blinked rapidly, processing his request. That was a problem with the mass-produced ones, they took their sweet time. It reminded him of the nannybot who'd looked after him as a baby. He had to clench his fists to stop himself from freaking out.

"Who sent you?"

Drat! It hadn't been looking up the numbers, it'd been trying to match his face with the museum human resources data file. He had to do something before it raised an alarm.

"Walker. Natalie Walker, owner of the building," he said, stepping back towards the doorway.

The android scratched its head. That meant he'd given it an answer that required more analysis. It gave him time to check out the corridor. The woman was gone, the coast was clear.

"Soz, got to go. I'll come and get them from you in a bit."

He was so busy escaping that he forgot to use the fake American accent. He was out of the door, headed to the stairway at the end when he heard the android raise the alarm.

"Security breach on level three!"

He sprinted down the stairs, two at a time. If he was right, there'd be a staff exit somewhere at the bottom and he could be out on the street before they caught him. He reached the ground floor, but the door off the stairs was locked and alarmed. It had a small glass panel through which he could see the marble entrance hall milling with people. So near, yet so far.

The clattering sound of fast-moving footsteps came echoing from above. Someone was after him. He turned and took the basement staircase, his Slider boots clanging noisily on the narrow, steel treads.

It took him down into a long, low, gloomy corridor that smelled musty and damp. There were rows of metal doors on each side, each one closed off with digital padlocks.

The footsteps were getting louder. It wasn't just one pair, it sounded like an army. He started to run, headed towards the other end. There had to be a way out.

He reached a fire door, but it too was locked.

His heart was now pounding in his chest. He was trapped.

Out of the corner of his eye he saw something silver coming hurtling towards him, like a streak of lightning. He jumped out of the way into the shadowed gloom, just in time for it to fly past. It crashed into the door, through it, and out the other side. Behind it came the unmistakeable dragon shape of Fizz, flapping his emerald wings, his eyes glowing bright amber. Nat followed, running at full pelt. None of them noticed him. He was expecting someone else to come chasing after them, but there was nothing.

As he peeked through a crack in the smashed door, he saw that the silver bullet that had shot past him was in fact a miniature, robotic goat.

"*I will deactivate if I leave the perimeter of the building, so my journey with you must end here,*" it said.

"*We can't leave you here, you're family,*" said Fizz.

The goat let out a long bleat. "*Sorry, that's how it goes. I'll be a desk object again when you leave the building, but if ever you come and visit I'll reactivate.*"

Zixin watched Nat reach out and stroke the goat's nose. "Thanks for all your help. We'll come back when we can. My grandfather would have been proud of you."

The goat's eyes flashed electric blue.

"You'd better scram. Good luck on Alcatraz."

Chapter Sixteen
FIZZ TO THE RESCUE

Nat couldn't be bothered to collect her Slider from the front entrance of the museum. She decided it'd be quicker to run all the way back to the hotel. The pig-lion might still be out there as well, maybe Zixin too, so it was best avoided anyway. She'd pick it up later.

She got Fizz to lead the way out of the side entrance, so that he could make sure the coast was clear. They came out on to a steep street. Below, she could see the fog-coated, grey waters of the Bay. Out there lay Alcatraz Island, the place that held the secret to the location of the sword. She was one step closer.

Fizz navigated back to the hotel. She jogged along behind him, her mind racing... Her grandfather had come to life on the screen, he'd said her name and talked to her. She'd never heard his voice before. It sounded laid-back but strong, and he had her eyes and mouth, just like her mum. How could he have had a heart attack only days afterwards?

And what about this great-great uncle who'd been

a prison guard on Alcatraz? It was yet more family history she didn't know. More big secrets.

Nat wondered why her mum had become so obsessed with the swords. She'd always thought it was her dad who was the one with the crazy ideas, building SPIN virtual worlds and games out of nothing but bits and bytes. But maybe it was really her mum?

The thoughts were tumbling and jumbling inside her. She pictured the goat walking along the corridor, on its way back to take its place on her grandfather's desk, as some labelled thing for tourists to gawp at again. She was determined that they'd go back and see it again. But first there was this sword business that she had to take care of…

She was so busy thinking and running that she didn't realise her breath was becoming raspy. Too late. It felt like someone had just lassoed her, and was pulling the rope tight around her chest.

"Ai yah, Fizz!" she cried, falling to her knees.

Her airways were closing. The steep, upward slant of the street started to blur. Stars danced in her vision. She heard the screech of brakes and felt a swoosh of air. Fizz landed next to her. He leaned over, putting his snout to her lips. She heard the click of the canister capsule inside him as he released her asthma medication. It came blasting into her mouth, traveling down into her lungs with a hurricane force. Her airways relaxed and she gulped in cool, salty air.

"Ma'am, ma'am, are you OK?"

A cable-car conductor wearing a brown uniform crouched down beside her, his hand on her shoulder. She nodded. She hadn't had an attack in a long while.

"*Her vital signs are normal again, thank you for your concern, kind sir,*" said Fizz, replying for her.

"Where are you headed?"

"*Nob Hill.*"

"Then at least let us take you up there," he said, offering her a hand.

Nat managed a weak smile and allowed him to help her up. The cable car had stopped next to where she'd collapsed on the pavement. It was packed with tourists and they were all staring at her, their faces full of pity. Her cheeks flamed with embarrassment.

"Here, Hank, move will ya! The girl can sit here with me," said a large woman in a baseball jacket and cap.

The guy stood up and helped Nat into his seat.

"*Thank you, kind sir,*" said Fizz.

"Hey, you're one polite creature. Never seen anythin' like your sort before," said the guy.

"I am a one-off, custom-built dragon, sir."

The woman put her arm around Nat's shoulders and gave her a squeeze.

"I gotcha," she said.

Fizz had to perch in Nat's lap. Nat wasn't so sure she wanted to be held, but the woman gripped on to her as the cable car moved off up the hill.

By the time they were dropped off, Nat felt normal again. The woman had talked to her the whole way, telling her about how they'd driven in their RV from Michigan all the way to San Francisco. She talked fast and loud, so all Nat had to do was listen and try to ignore the strong whiff of fried onions that came out with every word.

"If you talked like that all the time my databanks would overload," said Fizz, as soon as the cable car moved off.

They walked the last few steps to the hotel entrance. Nat was looking forward to getting back to her room, so that they could plan what to do next and get something to eat. Hopefully Henry had been able to keep Aunt Vera busy.

When the elevator doors slid open on to The Bullion Suite floor, she was expecting to find Hopkins waiting for them, but he wasn't.

Loud rock music was coming from behind the closed doors to the sitting room. It was accompanied by a woman, singing off-key, at the top of her voice.

"*I believe those are the dulcet tones of your aunt,*" said Fizz.

It couldn't be...

Nat stepped across the marble hallway, turned the brass knob, and peeked through a crack in the door. Expensive-looking shopping bags lay strewn around the room, designer dresses on hangers lay draped over the back of the sofas. There was a silver ice bucket with an open bottle of champagne on the mantlepiece, while her aunt stood on the gold coffee table wearing stilettos and a full-length black evening gown. She was using her half empty glass of champagne as a microphone, while Hopkins trotted around the table blasting out a rock tune from his head speakers, and playing air guitar. The noise was making the crystal chandelier above them shake.

By the window, Henry sat cross-legged on the floor with NutNut, keeping out of the way.

NutNut's head turned. It had detected Nat and Fizz. It swivelled around to Henry. He got to his feet and tiptoed unnoticed to the door.

"Tiger's teeth! I said to keep her distracted, but what

is she doing?" said Nat, once they were in her room.

Henry plonked himself down on the bed, his shoulders slumped.

"Mummy called Daddy but when he appeared on screen she freaked out. He's had a makeover, I saw it too, it's really *un-ku*. He's had red hairbots implanted to cover up his bald bits, and he's got a handlebar moustache, and is wearing one of those weird long velvet suits in green. And he was driving Jamuka's old Grooverider around London playing loud music from the last century. Worse still he had some floozy, well that's what Mummy said she was, sitting next to him. Daddy said it was his stylist and that Mummy shouldn't be so rude. Mummy screamed at him that he was 'having a mid-life crisis'. Daddy laughed and said Mummy should calm down. Mummy cut the call, and then we all had to go on a mad shopping spree with her. I didn't want to call you because you told me not to unless it was a life or death situation, but it has been really bad."

Chapter Seventeen
MARVICTOR

From where he was hidden in the shadows of the basement bar Zixin had watched the small goat trot back up the corridor. Alcatraz? Wasn't that some kind of old prison on a rock around here? Was that where the sword was hidden?

He'd then followed Nat and Fizz all the way back to their hotel. When he'd seen Nat collapse he'd wanted to run to help her, but he'd forced himself to hide in a doorway at the bottom of the hill, watching Fizz give her the medicine, and the cable car conductor give her a hand up.

The doormen kept looking over at where he was standing on the corner, giving him the evil eye. He was going to have to move on before they made him. And he couldn't go inside because he didn't have enough money to buy a drink. As if that wasn't bad enough, Scorta would soon be arriving to wait for Hopkins to come down with the latest report from The Bullion Suite.

There was only one solution. He'd have to break his promise to himself.

He set off downhill, making sure he was headed away from Chinatown. Hong knew a lot of people and he was sure his grandad had more robots than just Scorta roaming the streets. He crossed over Market and followed signposts for "South Park", the technology heart of San Francisco.

He reached a small square with a park in the middle, and went into the Grasshopper Cafe. It was packed inside with cowboys, cowgirls and geeks drinking cold brew coffee, all talking loudly at a million miles an hour. Their robots were sitting on the tables, joining in the chatter. Most of them were custom designed, like some zoo of weird creatures. He spotted a zebra-striped rat, a red goblin, and a golden bat all at the same table.

"*What can I get you today, sir?*" said a green grasshopper robot, who was standing behind the counter.

"A double shot cortado with a silicon wrapper," he said.

The grasshopper's antenna twitched. It reached under the counter, pulled out an old-fashioned credit card and passed it to him.

"*Door marked private next to the bathroom,*" it whispered.

He followed its directions and put the card into the lock. It clicked open and he was in. The Grasshopper Cafe was well-known in hacker circles. He'd known about it for years, and now he was here, going down a narrow, unlit winding staircase into the legendary Grasshopper basement.

The concrete walls and floor were painted black, ceiling spotlights lit rows of lime coloured, egg-shaped VR pods. Most of them were closed, with their digital panels showing they were already occupied, but he found a vacant one at the end. He climbed into the pilot seat, put on the goggles and helmet and hit the activate button. The egg closed. He could feel his heart begin to beat faster, his palms begin to itch.

"*Iris scan complete, identification verified. Welcome Marvictor.*"

His virtual universe spread out before him like a starlit galaxy. He flew over to the black hole he'd created and jumped in.

He worked quickly, and half an hour later he was done. Hack complete. He headed out, went straight to the nearest branch of The Golden Gate Bank, and walked up to the cashier's desk.

INDIGO ISLAND

The android bank teller smiled at him.

"*Good day Mister Troxbury. What can I do for you this fine day?*" it said.

"I need to take out five thousand dollars in cash," he said, sweat beading at the back of his neck, his stomach knotted with fear.

The last time he'd done this was when he'd been nine years old and discovered he was able to hack into the London Trust Bank. He'd created an account and stupidly given himself a million pounds. Within twenty-four hours he'd been tracked down by the London Met Police fraud squad. They'd broken down the door of his flat in the middle of the night and arrested him. He'd been too young to charge and send to prison, so instead they'd sent him off to a juvenile remand centre for five months. The other kids in there had made his life a misery. When he was finally set free he vowed to himself that he'd never rip off a bank again. Until now...

"*Certainly, sir. How would you like it?*"

"Twenty-dollar bills, please."

The android opened the cash drawer and started counting out the money in front of him. As the seconds ticked by and the stack grew he wished he'd asked for fifties. He could feel the lenses of the security cameras overhead focused on his every move.

"There you go, sir. Would you like an envelope?"

"Yeah, please, that would be great."

The android pulled a large brown envelope out of the drawer and put the notes inside. It then pushed the envelope into the tray under the cashier's window.

"Will that be all for you today, sir?"

He nodded, picked up the envelope and stuffed it inside his cowboy jacket.

"Well, you have a nice day, then!"

Zixin strode quickly out of the bank. The envelope felt like it was burning a hole in his jacket as he walked up the street. He felt sure that any moment now a security guard would come chasing after him with a pair of handcuffs, and drag him off to jail.

Once he reached the end of the block he took a left turn and broke into a sprint, running as fast as his legs would work. He wanted to put as much distance as he could between the bank and himself.

A few blocks further up he flagged down a GrooveCab.

"Can you take me to the terminal for the Alcatraz ferry, please?"

The raccoon-robot driver nodded.

"Sure, hop on in. The traffic is running smoothly so

should be a short ride today, sir."

He paid for his cab ride using one of the fresh, crisp, twenty-dollar notes from the envelope. It was already rush-hour and the Ferry Building he'd been dropped at was heaving with city workers and tourists.

He followed signs for boats to Alcatraz Island, but when he approached the ticket counter a seagull robot came swooping down, blocking his path.

"We're closed for the day. We open again at eight am tomorrow sir. Can I interest you in prepaying for the early 'Rock 'n Roll' boat and tour. It costs fifty-two dollars and includes a free breakfast pastry and hot drink of your choice," it squawked.

"Nah, I'll leave it, thanks," Zixin said, turning to walk out.

"I'll give you an extra ten percent off if you book now," said the seagull, following him.

He raised his hand.

"Not today."

"But sir, it's a one time special deal I'm..."

He stopped and spun around. The seagull was hovering in the air right in front of him.

"Get out of my space! Stay in your lane and let me get out of here."

His hand flew to his neck where Vesperetta would

normally be draped around him like a scarf. She would have thrown shade over this bot. She'd have hissed at it and told it to back off.

The seagull retreated. Zixin headed back outside and looked across to where Alcatraz Island loomed up from the slate-grey choppy waters of the Bay. An old lighthouse was sticking out of the middle of it into the evening sky, like some abandoned rocket on a rocky launchpad. Below it, perched on the summit of the island, stood a ghostly, square cell building. He shivered. Prisons weren't his kind of place.

He set off along the waterfront towards the Golden Gate Bridge. There had to be another way to get there. He passed the pier where he had bought his cowboy outfit earlier, and made his way to the next one along, where he could see rows of private boats moored up behind a security gate. Most of them were locked up, but on the far floating jetty he spotted a young guy in shorts and t-shirt onboard an old, single-masted sailboat. He was untying his ropes to cast off.

"Hey, excuse me!" he called, rattling the gate to get the guy's attention.

The guy shrugged. "There's plenty of tour cruisers up that-a-way."

He pointed back towards the Ferry Building.

"I know, but I like proper sailing, being low on the water, feeling the power of the wind. I've got cash and would pay well," he shouted.

The guy scratched his beard. "I'm only going out for an hour, how much would you be willing to pay?"

Zixin hadn't thought this bit out. He paused, wondering how much it would take.

"A hundred?"

The guy shook his head. "I'll take a pass on that, thanks. You have a good evening."

He turned his back and carried on untying the ropes. "Three hundred, I'll pay you three hundred dollars!" The guy paused, dropped the rope, jumped on to the jetty, and came jogging towards the gate. Zixin reached into his jacket and hurriedly counted out three hundred dollars in twenty dollar notes. He held them up for the guy to see. The guy opened the gate, took the offered cash.

"You've got yourself a deal, dude," he said, and shook his hand.

Chapter Eighteen
DISGUISE

The music and singing got louder. The drum beats and guitar chords shook and rattled the doors and windows as if they were trying to escape the sitting room.

Nat didn't care. It meant Aunt Vera was busy, and not bothering her. She and Henry had shut themselves in her room and were dining on a radically random selection of food items from their raid to Vera's minibar. Empty bags of mini pretzels, cookies, candy and crisps lay littered around the bed. They hadn't dared order room service because that would have disturbed Hopkins, and broken up the rock party.

Wen was on Fizz's diamond-def screen wearing her yellow sunflower helmet and Weiwood school uniform. She was cruising on her Slider, up The Peak in Hong Kong, on her way to school.

"Ai yah! So it's some old uncle who was a prison guard who started all this crazy sword stuff?" she said, after Nat had filled her in on the latest.

"Uncle Harold. Fizz has checked him out. Harold Drew was on Alcatraz for years. He lived out there even after it closed as a prison, and did the tourist tours."

Henry stopped crunching his way through his second bag of crisps. "And I got NutNut to check out Mad MacDuff. He was found next to a *dead man*, that was why he ended up in the prison. They said he killed him, but MacDuff said he never did but some judge said the evidence was irrefagular..."

"*Irrefutable! The evidence was irrefutable. That means it was beyond doubt!*" squeaked NutNut, flicking Henry's arm with its bushy tail.

Henry flicked its tail back. "Stop correcting me!"

"That's right, back off squirrel. You're interrupting us here," said Wen.

"NutNut shutdown!" shouted Henry.

"Attaboy, Henry, don't let your robot out-boss you," said Wen.

A big squeal came sounding out through Fizz's speakers.

"Cut it out, Fu!" shouted Wen.

Nat saw her reach out towards the screen. Fu would be perched on her Slider handlebars. Wen's parents had bought her a Soyto rabbit robot to help curb her sharp tongue, because Soytos were programmed to be highly sensitive to criticism. Nat smiled; she wasn't sure it had helped.

"Fizz got us tickets and we're booked on the first boat out to Alcatraz in the morning," said Henry, crunching more crisps and jumping up and down on the bed in excitement.

"And what are you going to wear? You can't go like that," said Wen.

Nat looked down at her Smart t-shirt. "Why not?"

"You need a disguise. If snake boy and the pig-lion thing are on your tail you'd better not be looking like you."

Zoinks, she was right! Nat had been so caught up in her family sword history, that she'd almost forgotten about slimy Zixin. She saw that Wen was passing through the tall iron gates to Weiwood. A pang of homesickness came bubbling up for her old school.

She glanced over at the bedside table, which was stacked with piles of SmartPapers – all of them homework. Henry had given them to her. He'd got a stack too. Apparently they'd arrived on his mother's FastPad, courtesy of Professor Trogalming at Boxbury School, and she'd got Hopkins to sort, print and distribute them.

"Is there a 3D printer in your lush suite?"

"Yep, I've seen one in the sitting room in that big gold desk. Are you going to make us some disguises? Can I be a cowboy?" said Henry, grinning.

Wen had reached the parking shelter and jumped off her Slider. Nat could hear the school bell's shrill ring in the background. A Weiwood school monitor robot appeared on screen.

"*Late again, Miss Tang. That's last bell and this is the third time this week. Report to the detention room at break.*"

"Give me a break will you and back off!"

"*That's a double detention.*"

It turned and whirred off on its wheels to track down other tardy pupils.

"This sucks! The new headmistress has got monitor robots everywhere, even in the loos. You're not missing anything here," Wen grumbled, taking off her helmet.

Nat wasn't so sure. She'd rather have a school monitor following her than a creepy lion-pig.

"Can I? Please can I be a cowboy?" whined Henry.

Wen started to run towards her classroom. "Let me check out what's on trend, you've got to blend in. I'll send Fizz the files. You get the printer hooked up in your room and make sure its got a load of multi-colour textile cartridges!"

Fizz's screen went blank. He folded in his wings. Nat looked over at the closed bedroom door, beyond which lay the sitting room. They needed to sneak into it somehow and get past the rock duo to get to the printer.

"Henry, do you still have that Sneaker Patrol app loaded in NutNut?"

He nodded. "It's the only way I can get midnight snacks when I need them."

Nat got up off the bed and retrieved the squirrel from the floor where it was lying on its back, paws in the air, eyes closed.

"Here, power NutNut up and get it to go into Sneaker Patrol mode and fetch the printer."

Henry pressed its nose. The squirrel's eyelids popped open. He gave it the instructions and set it off outside the bedroom door.

Five minutes later it returned, pushing the printer into Nat's room.

"*Message from Prissy. She wants you to call her immediately,*" it said, landing the printer at Henry's feet.

Henry bent down and picked it up. "Prissy?" he

said, frowning. "She never calls me."

Just hearing her older cousin's name made Nat shudder.

"She'd only call you if she wanted something. You'd better do it quick and get it over with otherwise you know what she's like, she'll call your mum and complain."

Henry sat down on the bed, frowning.

"She's on the other side of the world from us right now, so she's far away."

He took a big intake of breath.

"NutNut, call Prissy."

She answered immediately. Nat dodged out of the way of NutNut's camera so she wouldn't be seen.

"What is going on over there?!!" screamed Prissy.

She didn't give Henry time to respond because she went off on a long rant about how their mum had posted a video of herself dancing on a gold table in some hideous dress, drinking champagne out of the bottle, while she danced with a half man, half pony.

NewsAmp had picked it up, and it was now TRENDING in their "Lifestyles of the Rich" category. The shame of it! Loads of friends had seen it. She'd tried to call their mum but all calls were blocked.

Nat bit her lip, trying not to laugh. She'd never heard Prissy so furious before.

"It's because Mummy's cross with Daddy. She says he's having a mid-life crisis," said Henry, when Prissy had finally paused for breath.

Nat just had to have a quick peek.

"Show me Prissy," she whispered in Fizz's ear.

He swooped off her shoulder, landed behind NutNut, and peeked his snout around to the screen.

Nat could now see Prissy in all her fury and flouncy Victorian frills on Fizz's screen. She was surprised to see that she was standing in one of the Boxbury dorms.

"You've got to stop her Henry. NOW!"

Henry glanced at Nat. "Just tell her you will," she mouthed silently, drawing her hand across her neck to cut the call.

"OK, Prissy. I'll try."

Chapter Nineteen
THE ISLAND

The waters of the Bay were choppier than Zixin expected, colder too. He somehow had it in his head that because he was in California the water would be warm; instead it was freezing. He pulled the fringed jacket tighter around him. The sun had gone down and the wind kept changing direction, so the guy had to keep changing tack to navigate the small sailboat towards Alcatraz.

They didn't talk much so Zixin watched the dark shadowed cliffs loom closer.

"I'm not going to be able to get you in close enough to drop you on shore. Give me another hundred and I'll let you have my dinghy and you can row in if you're really that keen to get there tonight."

"From here?" said Zixin, seeing a huge expanse of dark swell between him and the rock.

The guy laughed. "I can take you in closer than this, just not all the way."

He reached into his jacket for the cash. Anything to

get a head start on the search before Nat arrived.

Twenty minutes later he was on his own in a kid's orange inflatable dinghy. It was only just big enough for him, and it sat very low on the water.

"Careful of the great whites!" shouted the guy, disappearing off back to the bright lights of the city.

Sharks. That was all he needed. Zixin dipped the flimsy plastic paddle into the dark water and began to propel the dinghy towards the island.

He soon broke into a sweat as he moved the paddle from one side to the other, trying to get a rhythm going. He kept imagining that at any moment a massive shark would surface, open its jaws, and gobble him up.

He wondered where Scorta was right now, and what his grandad was plotting. And Vesperetta, where was she? What had his grandad done to her?

It took all his strength to row the dinghy close enough to the rocks to be able to jump on to dry land.

The dinghy slipped back out into the Bay while Zixin stared up at the cliff face before him. There probably hadn't been many people wanting to break into this place; most would have wanted to escape. He began to climb and soon found Slider boots weren't made for climbing. They kept slipping on the wet rocks. The only thing that kept him going was the thought that this was the only way he was ever going to get Vesperetta back.

He crawled up and on to a pot-holed road. He lay for a moment catching his breath, grateful to be off the water. He had no way of knowing what time it was but he guessed that it had to be close to midnight.

He sat up and looked around him. The place was eerily deserted. He could only hear the wind and the waves. A group of buildings lay further up the rock, like some kind of ghost village. This island was way bigger than he'd imagined.

He got to his feet and started walking along the road. It wasn't long before he reached a junction where a signpost marked "*Cellhouse*" pointed upwards to the massive, dimly lit building at the summit. The other way was marked "*Building 64: Information Center*".

Information, that was a word he knew well. Information meant computers. He followed the sign down towards the water on the other side of the island. He was halfway along when he heard the crunch of wheels on gravel. A pair of headlights appeared around a corner. He ducked and threw himself into the scrubby undergrowth next to the road.

A patrol Overrider came crawling along. As it went by he could see that it had a raccoon security robot at the wheel. Its masked eyes were scanning the road in front. He held his breath and lowered his head. It passed on up towards the main cell house.

He waited for it to get out of sight before continuing on his way. This time, he was more wary and kept to the edge of the road.

Building 64 was part of a long old warehouse building next to the water. Its facade was lit by floodlights, so he kept to the shadows at the back of the building, looking for a way in.

Zixin tried the doors but they were locked. He was beginning to think he'd have to start somewhere else when he looked up and spied that a top floor window was cracked open.

Chapter Twenty
ALCATRAZ

Nat woke up to the sound of Fizz snorting like an angry bull. She opened her eyes to find him standing on the dressing table staring at himself in the mirror. He'd opened the curtains to let in the first pale light of day.

Zoinks, was she seeing things? She rubbed her eyes, wiping away the heavy sleep.

"*Wen's made me this!*" he said, blowing a stream of smoke out of his snout. But it wasn't his snout, it was a bright pink beak. He spread his wings. "*I look unding and undragon.*"

It was hard to know what to say since he was wearing a feathered blue and red parrot suit.

"Um, well, I didn't recognise you, which is the point," she said.

His head drooped. "*I am not a parrot, I'm a dragon. Why couldn't she make me a dragon cowboy? That's what you've got, and Henry too – ku, on-trend cowboy and cowgirl outfits. Why did she make me a parrot suit?"*

Nat slid out of bed and walked over to the stack of outputs from the printer. She'd gone to sleep with it whirring, and it was still going. A black and white neckerchief was emerging into the tray. She picked up a pair of shiny grey jeans and a dark blue satin shirt with beaded trim. As Fizz said, they were on-trend. She even liked them.

"Sorry," she said. "I know you don't think you look good, but you do look like a proper parrot robot, which is a great disguise."

The door burst open and Henry came running in, carrying NutNut. He was wearing his pyjamas, his red hair standing on end.

"Have I got my outfit?" he said.

He was on his way over to where she was standing at the printer when he spotted Fizz and stopped. He blinked a couple of times and scratched his head.

"Fizz? You're a p…"

"A parrot, yes I am a parrot," snapped Fizz, more smoke pouring out of his beak.

"You're going to have to stop the smoke," said Nat. "It'll give you away."

He snapped the beak shut.

"NutNut gets to be a raccoon."

Henry grinned. "And me?"

Nat held up a cactus patterned green shirt and blue jeans. Henry took them off her, along with the raccoon suit, and disappeared into the bathroom.

"See? Everyone gets a ding *disguise but me."*

She sighed, walked over and picked him up off the dressing table.

"You are the most handsome dragon in the whole world. No other dragon looks like you and I don't want you getting hurt, so to keep safe you're going to have to wear it."

His eyes changed into purple heart shapes. He reached up to kiss her on the cheek but was so unused to his beak that he pecked her instead.

"Ow!"

"Sorry."

Ten minutes later they were dressed in their outfits. As well as jeans and shirts they'd got hats, belts, jackets and boots. Wen had been very busy.

They didn't have to sneak out of The Bullion Suite because Aunt Vera was snoring, fully clothed in her evening dress on her bed, while Hopkins was in the sitting room, lying on the gold table, out of power charge.

They took the elevator to the ground floor and

passed by reception without anyone recognising them. Fizz had ordered a GrooveCab to take them to the museum so that they could pick up the flower-power Slider.

Nat pulled it out of the storage rack and activated it to hover.

"This is cool," said Henry, sitting on the back. "It's way more comfortable than the ones at home."

"It's a slug," she grumbled, pulling out into the main Slider lane, which led down to the Ferry Building.

She set it to cruising speed and moved along in the flow of morning traffic. They looked like locals now and blended in with the other riders on their wide boards. There were more cowboys, cowgirls, raccoons and parrots than anything else. Wen had got their disguises just right.

The Ferry Building was already teeming with people. Nat rode up to the valet Slider parking attendant and hopped off.

"You here for the full day, ma'am?" said the attendant.

"Yes, maybe even later, I'm not sure."

"OK. If you can get your parrot to scan this number you can call five minutes before you get back and we'll have your Slider ready and waiting."

Fizz snorted in disgust before scanning the number that flashed up on the valet's FastPad. He then hopped off the handlebars on to Nat's shoulder.

"*Parrot, he called me a parrot,*" he whispered.

"Shows your disguise is working," she whispered back.

There was already a long queue of tourists for the "Rock 'n Roll" boat. The line moved slowly while people *ummed* and *ahhed* over which complimentary warm pastry and drink to select before they boarded.

Henry didn't hesitate. He grabbed a giant sugar-glazed bear claw and a hot chocolate. Nat chose a cinnamon roll and green tea and they made their way up the stairs on to the open-air top deck, where they found a spot on a bench near the front of the ferry.

The whistle blew and the ferry rumbled into the Bay.

"It's not like the *Junko*, is it?" said Henry, biting into the bear claw.

Nat laughed. "No. It's *ku* to be on the water, though. I hate sleeping on dry land."

The salty, cool air tasted as good as the warm bun.

"When's the *Junko* going to get here?"

"Ah Ping sent a message last night. She's got the boat through the Panama Canal, and the MaxEdge engine is up to top sailing speed, so only a few more days."

Ah Ping might be able to sail the *Junko* single-handedly but she was a woman of few words. She only ever sent Nat very short messages, which she dictated into her FastPad. Nat had tried to call a few times to speak on video but the call always went straight to the automatic greeter. She couldn't wait for her floating home to get here!

"Can I stay with you on the *Junko?* I don't like the Tumnus thing, its creepy."

"You are right about Hopkins. It is a conflicted half android, half pony. It must feel like I do now. I am dragon inside, but now parrot outside. It is difficult to operate because my circuits are overloading with parrot behaviours," said Fizz, letting out a loud squawk.

Nat took a sip of green tea and looked over towards Alcatraz. No wonder they called it The Rock, because that was what it was, a huge chunk of grey rock sitting out in the indigo waters of the Bay. Concrete slab buildings covered its surface. Dotted between them were patches of green – scrub bushes and a few spindly pine trees that had found a way to grow amongst the stark, man-made landscape. A rusty water tower sat on one moss-covered building near the craggy shoreline.

INDIGO ISLAND

A tall, narrow chimney poked up out of another.

But it was the massive building at the top that dominated the view. If you took all the other buildings away you might be tricked into thinking it was some ancient palace with its columned walls and huge windows.

An old iron watchtower spoke of a different history. As the ferry drew closer the windows appeared more like dark hollows, punched out of the concrete, a view into a world of containment and punishment. A shiver ran up her spine. The worst of the worst criminals in America had been sent here, prisoners who were too dangerous to be put anywhere else.

The ferry docked at a jetty. They filed off down a gangway towards a long building with a balcony.

"*Welcome to the old United States Penitentiary, Alcatraz Island!*" said a ranger android, dressed in a brown uniform.

"This place looks scary," said Henry, grabbing on to Nat's arm.

Chapter Twenty-One
PEAGLE

Zixin's grandfather, Lang Liu, sat on his perch while Hong fitted the pug-dog head mask. He held his breath while Hong pulled the Spider-wire reinforced mask up and over his head. It snapped on. The nano-threads and sensors moulded on to his skull. Ever since his sickness had started all those years ago, he'd had to adjust to being encased in things that disguised his disfigured, failing body.

His head was the only part that still looked relatively normal, but now because of his wretched grandson going it alone, he was forced to put on the mask to go into the outside world and hunt down the girl himself.

For the millionth time he wished he'd been more careful with the everlasting-life experiment. Hong had warned him of the side effects of the injections, but he hadn't listened. He'd got too ambitious and taken five times the normal dose of the drugs. He was lucky to have survived.

"Is it done?" he said, impatience rising in him like

a red wave.

Hong's face was close to his own. His brows were knitted in concentration as he connected the mask to the bird body.

"Nearly."

"Well, get it done! Scorta, what news?"

The guinea-lion was sitting on its haunches next to the consulting-room door. It was only just back in his favour since it had returned with the news that the girl had picked up the Slider and was on the boat to Alcatraz.

"The Rocketboat awaits us at the pier," it said.

Hong stepped back, his head tipping left, then right as he checked the end result.

"We are done."

Lang Liu spread his wings and swooped down on to Scorta's shaggy head. He gripped its fur.

"Stay here until I contact you again. Get moving, Scorta, we've got work to do."

The guinea-lion stood up and trotted into the alleyway. It slipped into the Slider lane and started to accelerate, its paws drumming along the road. Passersby turned to gawp. Sliders swerved when their riders spotted the guinea-lion and Peagle. Lang Liu smiled behind his mask, enjoying the attention. Wait until he'd got a whole hybrid army of living robots behind him, then he'd make them kneel. And he would be their fearless leader. He would use the power of the swords to bond his body to his bird shell. They'd become one living creature.

Scorta ran all the way to the pier and pounced on to the deck of the waiting Rocketboat. The driver jumped in alarm when she saw who her passengers were and her hands shook as she took the wheel. Lang Liu liked that. Intimidating people gave him a real buzz. Hybrids scared humans. He saw it in the way their eyes tracked over him, trying to make sense of what they were seeing. The power lay in their fear.

As the Rocketboat moved into open water, he swooped off Scorta's head on to the guest seat next to the driver. He smiled when he saw her flinch.

She opened up the throttle. The hydrogen power cells unleashed their energy, sending the cigar-shaped speedboat rocketing across the surface of the choppy Bay. It dodged around the ferry boats, eating up the short distance to the island's jetty.

The engines slowed and they motored up to the VIP landing zone.

"An interesting place to keep America's most dangerous villains. They could see the city but they could never reach it. A tortuous position to be in, wouldn't you say?" said Lang Liu to the driver.

"Yeah, I guess so," she said, pulling the Rocketboat up to the jetty.

He hopped back on to Scorta's head. Scorta leaped on to the island before the VIP android attendant could put the gangplank in place.

The Rocketboat driver opened the throttle and roared off back to the city as fast as she could.

Chapter Twenty-Two
DRAGON-NAPPED

Nat and Henry were standing in the very cell that Ulysees MacDuff had occupied. It was on the upper level of the block, with a high, barred window. An old iron bed frame sat against one wall with just enough room for a small sink and toilet at the end. A rusty pale green table was fixed to the opposite wall.

"Want to see how it feels to be incarcerated?" said an android ranger, appearing outside in the corridor.

"Sure," said Nat, sitting down on the edge of the bed frame.

They'd finished the island audio tour, had walked forever, tramping from one building to another, and her feet were sore from the cowboy boots.

The ranger pulled the flat-strap iron bar door across. It clanged shut with a chilling, echoing finality.

She rubbed her temples. Her brain hurt from trying to figure out where MacDuff could have hidden the sword.

"The most famous occupant of this particular cell

was mad Ulysees MacDuff. They say he killed a man and was found sittin', rantin' next to the body. According to the prison reports he talked to himself day and night, used to drive the other prisoners in the nearby cells crazy," said the ranger.

"What did he talk about?" she asked, hoping for some clue, some nugget of information, that would lead them to Gan Jiang.

"Weird stuff about needin' to unite some ancient swords, that's what the reports say."

"I'm tired, can we go back to the hotel?" said Henry.

The ranger started to pull back the cell door.

"No, stop! Please can we stay in here a bit longer?" asked Nat.

The ranger dropped his hand from the door.

"Sure thing. Holler when you're good and ready. You've got ninety minutes left before the last ferry of the day," it said, heading up the corridor.

Henry dropped his backpack on to the bare concrete floor and sat on it.

"It's freezing in here. Can't we just go back now?" he moaned.

She looked over at her little cousin. He'd been really enthusiastic for most of the day. She'd put him in charge of filming and recording with NutNut. The squirrel's eyes were now half shut. It needed a power-up, and it looked like Henry did too.

"How about we check this cell out properly and then get the next ferry back. I'll buy you a Slamburger in the Ferry Building."

Henry managed a smile. "*Ku!*"

Nat looked around the bare walls. The green paint was flaking off, exposing the rough concrete beneath. When MacDuff was in here he must have had things to put on the shelf above the sink. Maybe some books from the library, a notebook, a cup. The wind came whistling in through the upper window. Rat's tails. This had to have been a terrible place to pass your time, even if you were mad.

Weirdly, though, she felt quite safe, probably because they'd escaped from Aunt Vera and Zixin. Henry had left a message for his mum saying they'd booked a day trip on a GrooveBus tour around San Francisco. No one knew they were on the island.

"Excuse me, would you be able to tell me whose cell this is?"

She looked over to the cell door but there was no one there.

"*Look!*" said Fizz, hopping off the bed and clacking across the floor on his talons.

She followed his direction. A large pug-dog head with big round eyes was peeping in from the far corner. It had a sandpapery, low gruff voice.

"*Mad Ulysees MacDuff,*" said Fizz.

"Ah, would you know why he was mad?"

Henry spotted the pug and perked up.

"I like pugs. I wanted a pug instead of a squirrel but Soyto only had chihuahuas in the small dog range. But you're a big pug, what make are you?"

NutNut's eyes snapped open. It flicked its tail in Henry's face and hissed. The pug let out a small whine, the kind that said "thank you for noticing me".

"I'm not really a pug, I'm a peagle, made by Batcan. There aren't many of us around because no one wanted us."

"What? How could someone not want you?" said Henry, getting up off his backpack, leaving NutNut watching him with its beady eyes, paws folded across its chest.

The peagle sniffed, its eyes became watery. Nat hadn't seen anything like it before. It was as if someone had taken a pug and blown it up to ten times its size.

"I'm unusual."

"How?" Henry stuck his hand through the bars and stroked its head.

Fizz poked his parrot head out. A long stream of smoke shot out of his beak.

"*You're not all pug!*" he said.

A big tear brimmed up and rolled down its cheek.

"It doesn't matter, peagle. Don't be mean, Fizz," said Henry.

Nat got up off the bed just as the peagle appeared in its entirety. She gasped. The pug bit was only its head, the rest was giant eagle.

"Henry, come here a sec will you, please?" she said, trying to sound calm.

But just as she said it the pug opened its mouth and bit him.

"Owww!" he howled, snatching his hand away.

Fizz didn't hesitate, he launched himself through the bars at the peagle, flames firing out of his beak. But the peagle lifted its massive clawed talon and grabbed him, squashing his parrot-feathered wings to his sides and clamping his beak shut.

"Noooooo!" cried Nat, jumping to the cell door to tug it open. But the peagle used its other claw to slam it shut, turn the old rusty key and pull it out of its lock.

It spread its wings and took off, flapping up the interior of the cell block. Tourists screamed as it flew overhead and out of an open upper window.

"Let me out!" screamed Nat, rattling the bars. "Let me out! Please let me out!"

It had taken her dragon. She shook the cell bars as a tsunami of panic came crashing down on her. The ranger came running to her aid. It tried to slide back the door.

"The key is gone. I have to go get the master one."

"My dragon, the bird thing's got my dragon in its mouth. You've got to stop it. PLEASE!" She was sobbing, shaking the bars.

"Ma'am, please be calm, first I've got to get y'all outta here. The boy's bleedin'," it said, running off up the corridor.

"No! You've got to stop the bird. Please! Please!"

"Nat, I'm so sorry, it's all my fault," said Henry, crying and clutching his bleeding hand.

She'd been so stupid. How could she ever think they were safe? Why, why did she ask to stay in here? And Fizz, why did she ever make him wear the stupid parrot costume? If he hadn't been in it he'd have been able to use his wings to escape the peagle's claws. The thought of losing him was more than she could bear.

"LET ME OUT!!" she screamed.

Her airways tightened. She clutched her hand to

her chest.

"Henry, I can't br—"

She blacked out, her head hitting the edge of the iron cot as she fell.

Chapter Twenty-Three
TEAMING UP

Nat could hear the low drone of city traffic. A hand brushed across her forehead. Someone was whispering close by, but she couldn't make out what they were saying. She twitched her nose and took a deep breath. A cool flow of oxygen came rushing in, whooshing down into her lungs like a winter's breeze.

Something was pressing on her face, around her mouth, across the bridge of her nose. She reached a hand up. Her fingers touched on something smooth. She traced over its bubble-shaped surface to her skin, to an elastic band that ran across her cheek. An oxygen mask.

When she tried to lift her eyelids it was as if someone had stuck lead weights on them. She tried focusing her mind, mustering up the energy to force them open.

She was looking up at a white ceiling decorated in gold-leaf stars. A face appeared over hers. She widened her eyes in shock and tried to move her head out of the way, but was stunned by a bolt of pain.

"Darling girl, you've had a nasty time of it. Don't move," said Aunt Vera, trying to frown beneath the rigid, smoothing Cementer layer.

A man with silver, curly hair and brown eyes moved into her place.

"Hey, Natalie. I'm Doctor Hutchinson. You've had a nasty bump to your head, along with an asthma attack. We've stabilised your breathing, but you've got to stay still and not move. OK?"

She blinked but then the memory of what had happened on Alcatraz came rushing back like a freight train.

"Fizz!" she cried, ripping the oxygen mask off and trying to sit up.

The doctor put his hand on her shoulder, gently but firmly pushing her back on to the pillow.

"I'm sorry, Nat, we don't know." It was Aunt Vera speaking, her voice soft and kind for once. "The paramedics flew you and Henry off Alcatraz. NutNut came too, but I'm sorry, they said there was no sign of your dragon."

Burning tears welled up. She curled up into a ball, hugging her knees. No Fizz? It was like a part of her had been cut off.

"You must rest, Natalie," said the doctor.

She felt a sharp prick on her arm. The jab of a needle. Then her world went dark.

"Nat? Nat?"

She opened her eyes. This time the room was lit by a bedside lamp, which cast a warm glow across the star ceiling. She turned her head, careful not to do it too quickly like the last time. Henry was sitting next to the bed, holding her hand. His small hand was bandaged. His face was white, pale as a ghost.

Behind him she saw an open wardrobe filled with dresses on hangers, their price tags still attached. She was in her aunt's bedroom in The Bullion Suite.

"They gave me a rabies injection and I've been sick, but I'm all right now. Are you? I thought you were going to die in the cell. You went all blue and there was blood coming out of the back of your head. The ranger got the medical kit just in time. I'm sorry, it's all my fault," he said, beginning to cry.

"Fizz? What happened?"

Henry snuffled and sniffed. "The peagle got away in a Rocketboat. That pig-lion thing you'd talked about was with it."

"What? You mean the peagle knows the pig lion? Was Zixin there?"

He shook his head. "I'm really sorry, Nat. You can

have NutNut."

NutNut jumped on to the bed. It put its paw on her arm and its eyes glowed bright blue.

"NutNut's yours."

Nat pushed herself up, fighting the throbbing in her head. If Zixin was part of this then she had something to go on, a lead somehow.

Loud voices erupted from down the hallway. They were followed by the thundering sound of hooves and boots on marble. Seconds later, Hopkins burst into the room with Zixin in hot pursuit.

Zixin launched himself through the air in a flying kick and caught Hopkins on the back of its head. The pony man fell to the floor. Zixin sprang on top of it but before he could land Hopkins lifted its hooves and kicked him, propelling him through the air and into the balcony window with such force that the glass shattered. The noise of car horns, sirens and cable car bells echoed up from the streets down below.

Nat groggily tried to climb out of the bed. She'd get Zixin for this.

Hopkins trampled through the broken glass and on to the balcony. It was about to kick Zixin with its pointy hoof, when Zixin's hands shot up, grabbed its leg and pulled it off its feet, up into the air. It went flying over the balcony and into the dark night.

"*Arrrrrrgggggggghhhh!*" it screamed as it plummeted down the side of the hotel.

There was a *thunk* and then silence.

"Where's my dragon?" screamed Nat, trying to run across the soft carpeted floor of the master bedroom. But her legs gave way beneath her.

"What have you done to my Hopkins?" cried Aunt Vera, running through the door, her stilettos crunching on shards of glass as she headed towards the balcony.

Zixin was up on his feet, dodging her clawing hands.

"Hopkins works for my grandad! He was sent to spy on you!" he shouted, trying to fend her off.

"What? Who is your grandfather? And why does he want to spy on us?" said Vera.

"Lang Liu. He's after Nat's swords, Mo Ye and Gan Jiang. He needs them to bring his robot army to life to take over the world."

Aunt Vera tittered with laughter. "How ridiculous."

Fuelled by a boiling anger, Nat forced herself to get to her feet.

"You took my dragon!" she screamed, taking another run at him.

She caught Zixin by surprise with a one-inch punch. He fell to his knees, clutching his stomach. She raised a hand, ready to chop him at the neck.

"Stop! I didn't, that's why I'm here!" he said, keeping his head bowed. "My grandad's got Vesperetta prisoner too, just like Fizz. He'll only let them go if we bring him the swords."

"What makes you think I believe that? This could just be another trick, like when you ran off with Mo Ye in Cornwall, you vile, fork-tongued liar!"

"I was forced to do that by my grandad. But then I came here and saw who he really was, that bird monster. I said I wouldn't help him any more, and then he took Vesperetta away and implanted a nano dot tracker in my ear. Look!"

He lifted his head and showed her his taped-up ear. It looked red and swollen. Something was oozing out from the side of the tape.

"It's in there, it buzzes in my head all the time. I had to fill up my ear with honey to stop it transmitting."

Nat lowered her hand.

"Why should I ever believe you?"

"I was on Alcatraz. I was in the visitor centre when Grandad flew overhead with Fizz in his claws. People were screaming. I tried to get outside, to stop him, but he escaped on a Rocketboat before I could get to him. That's why I'm here. We both need our robots back and we've got a better chance of us doing it together."

"No way."

Aunt Vera clapped her hands together. "This sword business sounds like a lot of nonsense."

Nat turned on her aunt. "It is not nonsense! People have died because of them. Maybe you should stop helping yourself to my fortune and start thinking about something other than yourself for once!"

Her aunt stamped her foot, turned on her heel and stormed out of the bedroom, slamming the door behind her. Nat's head started spinning. She took a step back and had to sit down in a chair. Zixin moved to her side.

"I know you hate me. I'd feel that way too if you'd done the same to me. But the only way we're going to get our robots back is if we team up."

Chapter Twenty-Four
LOCKED UP

Lang Liu prodded the dragon with a talon. It didn't move. He unplugged it from the power drainer. It'd taken the whole night to get to this point. It was a feisty robot with such a high security threshold that even he, robot maker and brilliant mind, could not access it.

Once they'd wrestled it out of the parrot suit he discovered that the whole body was SmartSkinned, able to repel the sharpest of instruments. He'd had to get Hong to tie it down with a Spiderwire mesh secured with nano-anchors, and to tape up its fiery snout with flameproof tape. It'd already singed a couple of his feathers. It was a tricky, vicious robot. The only solution had been to power drain it, and all of this had to be done in a blackout sphere so that it couldn't communicate with the outside world.

"Lock it in the safe with the snake. Then get me pugged up. When Scorta gets back from meeting Hopkins we'll go back out to Alcatraz. Has the ranger been bribed?"

Hong nodded. "My nephew is taking the cash out now on the first ferry. It'll be sorted by the time you arrive."

Lang Liu stretched his wings out and yawned.

"I must rest. When Scorta appears send it in."

Hong carried the blackout sphere containing the dragon out of the consulting room. Lang Liu heard him flick the light switch and head down the creaky wooden stairs to the basement. He had both robots now. The girl and Zixin were so attached to them they'd do anything to get them back, and that was where he needed them to be.

He flew over to his perch on the rail and hooked himself up to his nutrient and waste processor. The machine hummed into action. He closed his eyes and fell into a deep sleep.

"*Lang Liu, It's Scorta. I bring news.*" The guinea-lion's words brought him back to consciousness.

"Go ahead," he said.

"*Hopkins did not attend our meeting on the steps of the Cathedral at the scheduled time. I waited a further hour before contacting our mole at the hotel. I have intelligence that Hopkins is deceased. It fell from The Bullion balcony last night and smashed to smithereens on Pine Street. The Cable Car company cleared it off the cable tracks and transported the remains to the municipal recycling centre on Bush Street."*

"They took Hopkins for recycling? Who killed it?" he roared, now fully awake.

That pony-man hybrid had taken months to design and build. It had been expensive too. He'd make sure that hotel paid for its demise during work hours.

"Hard to ascertain. There was a report of a smashed balcony window but the hotel manager dealt with the matter himself, and has hushed the incident up."

"And Zixin?"

"Nothing yet."

He'd turn up soon enough, of that Lang Liu was certain. Hong walked in carrying a bowl of steamed duck dumplings.

"Bring them straight over."

Hong walked across to the perch and pulled a pair of gold chopsticks out of his top shirt pocket. He picked out a dumpling. Lang Liu wolfed it down.

"Keep them coming," he said, plum sauce dribbling down his chin.

"Now that we have lost Hopkins you'll have to go and work with our mole at the hotel, Hong. Monitor all activity at The Bullion Suite. We won't be able to get past hotel sweeper security, so it'll be eyes and ears. See if you can get a room service call. We'll be on the island looking for the sword."

He spoke while he chewed and chomped through the dumplings. Bits of dough and duck flew out, landing on the linoleum floor.

"Any update on the container ship?"

"Tomorrow, four fifty-two pm," said Scorta.

Lang Liu smiled at the thought of all the modified hybrid guinea-lions that were on the ship. It wouldn't be long now.

Chapter Twenty-Five
OPERATION

Nat lay staring into the shadowy darkness of the bedroom. She'd been evacuated from Aunt Vera's while they fixed the balcony window and had moved back into the tiny staff room. She couldn't sleep because every time she closed her eyes she pictured Fizz being grabbed in that vile peagle's claws and it flying off with him. And it wasn't even a robot. According to Zixin it was his grandad dressed up in some weird suit. She should never have asked to be left in the cell. She'd never, ever forgive herself.

And where was her dragon now? Where had he been taken to? All she wanted was to get him back. She'd give anything, do anything...

She swung her legs out of the bed and headed into the hallway. At least she wouldn't have to deal with the sneaky Hopkins any more. She made her way to the sitting room to get a cold Popko juice from the minibar.

The lights were already on when she opened the door, and she found Zixin lying on one of the sofas.

"What are you doing?" she said, getting a can from the fridge.

"Can't sleep because my ear is killing me. "

He lifted his head. Underneath she saw he'd wrapped ice cubes up in a napkin. The cloth was spotted with blood. His face was covered in a sheen of sweat.

"The buzzing's doing my head in. Please can you take a look?"

She went over and checked it out. There was smelly green stuff oozing out of his ear canal.

"Rat's tails, that's bad!" she said, covering her nose and mouth with her hand.

He might be her sworn enemy but she wouldn't wish that infection on anyone.

"What do I do? I can't get a doctor 'cos they'll clean it up, and then Grandad will know where I am."

Nat stepped back and took a long slurp of Popko juice. She might not be feeling great, but he was in a much worse state then her. He was also her only link to his grandad, who had Fizz.

"I'll be back in moment."

She snuck into Henry's room. He was sound asleep

in his bed with NutNut on the pillow next to him. She carefully reached over and grabbed the squirrel, whisking it out of the room before it woke up out of sleep mode.

She ran to her bedroom and locked them both in the bathroom. NutNut's eyes snapped open. Before it could start complaining about being kidnapped she clamped her hand over its mouth.

"Don't say a word. I am overriding your security access feature with password 'Fizztasticflyingdragonsquashessquirreltalk'," she said, using the code Fizz had created to deal with the squirrel when it got too full of itself.

NutNut's eyes flashed bright blue. She removed her hand.

"Contact Philippe using code 'NBC911'."

In a matter of seconds, her dad's old engineer appeared on NutNut's tail screen. He'd had a haircut since she'd last seen him in London. It was a radical one that made him look like a hedgehog with brown and red short spikes.

"Natalie! How is San Francisco? Have you found Gan Jiang?" he said, the moment he saw her.

Immediately she felt less panicked. If anyone knew what to do it was Philippe.

She told him everything. It took a while because he kept butting in and asking questions. She thought he would know about the silver goat, but he had no idea of its existence. But when she told him that Lang Lilu was Zixin's grandad, he exploded.

"*Mon Dieu!* That snivelling hybrid robot-maker is snake-boy's grandad?! Many years ago he tried to bring down SPIN, and get your dad to give up his company. He got some hackers to break into our systems and cause chaos. We got them out, of course, but it took time and they did a lot of damage. I bet that's how he found out about the swords!"

He was so cross that his thick-framed glasses had steamed up.

"And now he's got Fizz," said Nat.

There was a loud thud as Philippe slapped his hand down on his desk.

"We must find a way to stop him, and get back your dragon!"

"I know, but how?"

Philippe scratched his head. "First, we need to sort out snake boy."

Nat wrapped a t-shirt around her nose and mouth to block out the bad smell, but it still permeated through the fabric and made her gag.

She'd set up a makeshift operating theatre to perform the nano-dot extraction from Zixin's ear. He was lying on the dining table under the harsh glare of a desk lamp, while she used NutNut's Spiderwire to fish down through the honey and pus to locate it. Philippe had shown her how to disconnect one of the squirrel's tiny ear cameras, and one of its micro-magnets from a paw, and attach them to the end of the wire. It'd been a tricky job, partly because NutNut kept trying to bite her while she removed the camera and magnet, and partly because it was very hard to see what she was doing.

It was all tiny stuff, so she'd had to sneak into Aunt Vera's room and get her FastPad so that she could use its micro-magnifier. Luckily, though the window had been fixed and her aunt was snoring in the bed, she hadn't woken up. She checked the FastPad screen, which was hooked up to the camera. It showed it navigating though a pink and red sea.

Zixin's eyes were squeezed shut. He hadn't said a word since she'd started. She couldn't work out if it was because of the long, angry lecture from Philippe or because the pain had reached overload.

Maybe it was both.

If Jamuka had been here, he'd have known what to do. A few acupuncture needles stuck in the right places, some ancient remedy from the medicine cupboard on the *Junko*, and Zixin wouldn't be feeling a thing…

Chapter Twenty-Six
PHILIPPE

Nat flushed the toilet one more time to be totally certain.

"Nat, have you got an upset tummy? Have you got NutNut in there?"

It was Henry, knocking on the bathroom door. She finished rinsing her hands and opened the door.

He was standing in his pyjamas, yawning. The first few strands of daylight were coming in through the gap in the bedroom curtains. It'd been a long night.

"No. I was flushing away the nano dot from Zixin's ear. It's deactivated and on its journey out of here."

Henry scratched his head. "*Ku*. How did you get it out?"

"Long story, but I had to borrow NutNut to give me a hand."

He bit his lip. "Because you didn't have Fizz."

She put her arm around his shoulders and steered him out of the door towards the sitting room.

"Your squirrel did a top job. I had to borrow a

couple of things off it, but I'll let you put them back."

They walked in to find Zixin still lying on the dining table, so that his ear could drain into the folded towel that she'd laid out for him. He looked a bit less green and sweaty, which was a good sign, and he was talking quietly to Philippe on NutNut's tail screen. Henry ran over while she went to the mini bar and grabbed another Popko juice, and a packet of cookies. She'd have ordered something from room service but ever since Hopkins she didn't trust anyone coming up to the suite. It was bad enough knowing her aunt was only a couple of rooms away, but at least she knew what her aunt was like. All she wanted was money and a mansion. But people like Lang Liu wanted much more, and they'd kill to get it.

She joined the others at the table. Henry was sitting next to Zixin's head, leaning over so that they could both see Philippe on the screen.

"My grandad'll defo be on Alcatraz right now, you can guarantee it. He and Scorta'll be searching in places that've never been searched before. We've got to get back there before he finds Gan Jiang, otherwise we're all done for 'cos he's got a ship full of unlicensed hybrid robots arriving, a whole army of them. With them and the sword, we'll all be toast," said Zixin.

"Ah, Natalie, you are back," said Philippe, seeing her. "These hybrids make me very worried."

"I've been thinking, can you reprogram the goat so it can leave the museum without being deactivated?" she said, crunching a cookie.

Henry reached over and grabbed one out of the bag.

"My hunch is that since your dad designed it, its core construction is like Fizz, so perhaps I can."

"*Ku*, because we need it."

Philippe scratched his head. "I'd need you to go to the museum, so that it activates, and then you call me."

She looked over at her aunt's rolled-up FastPad. Its recharge light had finally turned green. Emerald green like Fizz. She badly needed her dragon back.

"I'll take the Slider and call you."

She was about to get down off the table but Zixin grabbed her arm.

"Hang on. You need to take the tracker off it before you go anywhere. Scorta knows its number and it'll trace you." She sighed.

"Soz. My fault," he said.

Forgiveness was a tricky thing. One moment she wanted to punch him, the next she remembered that his grandad used him like a puppet.

"Can I come with you?" said Henry, spraying cookie crumbs from his overstuffed mouth.

She shook her head. "You stay here and look after Zixin."

"We'll use NutNut to do some research on Alcatraz," said Zixin.

"What about Mummy?"

Nat shrugged. "If she ever comes out of her room again, tell her I said she should go shopping, spend as much money as she likes, but just keep out of my way."

Zixin whistled. "Flexin' and savage."

She glared at him and stalked out of the room.

Nat didn't need a map to get her to her grandfather's old house, she could have got there blindfolded. It was so early that the street in front was deserted, so she rode all the way up to the front entrance, right to the doors.

Once again she lifted the heavy brass knocker and let it bang down on the door.

"Yeah, yeah," came a voice on the other side.

She heard the bolts draw back and the same guard appeared. The moment he saw her his eyes popped wide open and he swiftly opened the door to let her in. As he was busy trying to salute her and say "Welcome back Miss Walker", the familiar sound of thundering hooves came echoing down the stairs.

Seconds later, in a flash of silver, the goat appeared at her feet. The guard ran off, back to his office.

"Well howdy, Natalie. Where's Fizz?"

She was relieved to see it. Somehow in all the madness its goaty, no nonsense attitude made her feel safe. Maybe it was because it had belonged to her grandfather. She gave it the update. The goat snorted and stamped its hooves on the marble.

"That ain't right. Let's get your Philippe guy on the line and get me outta here fast. Follow me."

The goat turned and trotted off up the stairs. She followed it up, along the corridor and into her grandfather's old office. The goat shut the door behind them and warm air started blasting out of the ceiling vents.

Nat sat down in the old leather armchair at her grandfather's oak desk and laid out the FastPad. She called Philippe. He appeared holding a giant mug of steaming coffee. He was yawning, but when he saw the goat he ripped off his glasses, leaned into camera and grinned.

"Mon Dieu. You are a very fine specimen of Max Walker's work!"

Chapter Twenty-Seven
BARBURY GRANT

Nat leaned forward on the handlebars and took the Slider up to its top cruising speed as they climbed Nob Hill. The goat was so excited to be free it was standing on the back of the board singing at the top of its voice. So much for staying incognito as they glided up to the hotel entrance.

The doorman took her Slider.

"Thanks, buddy, but keep it ready and waiting, will ya?" said the goat, head-butting the hotel door open before any staff could get there first.

It trotted across the foyer as if it owned the place, straight to The Bullion Suite lift. People were staring, so Nat kept her head down and ran in its wake.

"Can we please try to keep a low profile?" she said, as the lift doors closed.

They reached the top floor and headed into the sitting room. The blinds were down, and it was dark inside. NutNut was projecting an Alcatraz tour on the wall screen.

"Hey y'all. Good to make your acquaintance," said the goat, springing on to the coffee table next to NutNut.

It gave the squirrel a high-five, nodded over at the sofa where Henry was sitting, and turned to check out the film.

"Where's Zixin?" said Nat, flicking on a table lamp.

Henry pointed to the door. "He's gone for a shower in my room. His clothes smell really bad, like someone died in them, so I called Wen and asked her to make him some new ones. She said she had to talk to him first, and they had a big argument. Wen told him he was a slimy, *un-ding* snake, and other stuff too, but I shouldn't say exactly what those words were because I'm not meant to know them. He had to grovel and promise that he'd never do anything to hurt you ever again, otherwise Wen was going to hunt him down. I had to plug in NutNut's power-up because they talked for so long."

Nat frowned. "And how did it end?"

"OK, I think. The printer's still in your room and it's busy printing some stuff. Wen wants you to call her."

She'd do that, but later. That would be a big

conversation about trust and Zixin, and right now she didn't need that. He was her key to getting Fizz back.

She sat down on the sofa, sinking into the warm, velvet cushions. The dark room, the slow-moving film... A wave of tiredness swept over her and her eyelids grew heavy...

"Nat, Nat, wake up!"

She jolted out of a deep sleep to find Henry shaking her shoulder.

"Look!"

She turned her head on the cushion. NutNut was lying down, asleep on the coffee table, hooked up to a Spiderwire power-up, while the goat had taken over the show. It was projecting a photo showing a bald prisoner sitting at his desk holding a paintbrush.

"Wicked, you're awake," said Zixin, appearing from behind the sofa.

She rubbed her eyes, not sure if she was dreaming. He was wearing a Smart t-shirt with a photo of Fizz glowing bright emerald on the front. Below it, written in gold, it read *"I owe this dragon big time."* His slider trousers were covered in shimmering green dragon scales.

"Wen's idea?" she said.

He nodded, put his hands in his pockets. "Yeah. We did a deal."

She pushed herself up.

"*Ku*, she's right, you do owe him big time."

He lowered his eyes, shuffled further forward, and sat on the arm of the sofa.

"Yeah, I know that. You too. Thanks for fixing my ear."

"LOOK!" shouted Henry.

He was now standing in front of the screen pointing to a half-painted canvas propped up against the cell wall. It showed an outline of the Golden Gate Bridge. At the top of the canvas, on the edge, where it stretched over the wooden frame, the name "*Barbury Grant*" was handwritten in pencil.

"What about it?" said Nat.

"Pull up the visitor centre photo of MacDuff's cell," said Zixin.

The photo of his sparsely inhabited cell appeared on screen. Her stomach flipped as her mind flashed back to Fizz being dragon-napped.

"Zoom in on the pillow," he said.

The pillow looked grey and pixelated as the goat zoomed in. Nat saw immediately there was something underneath, a canvas faintly scrawled with the name

"*Barbury Grant*".

She got up and walked closer to the screen. Why had MacDuff got a painting under his pillow?

"Is it a painting of Gan Jiang?"

"That's the sticky bit. We can't find any paintings done by Barbury," said Zixin.

"Who was he?"

The goat switched off its projector-mode and turned to her.

"*Barbury Grant (January 6, 1918–December 12, 1962) was one of America's most infamous outlaws. He is known as the Golden Gate Bank Robber. During his criminal career, he stole over $1,000,000 in cash and securities. He was the most dangerous inmate in the history of Reno Prison and he was dubbed by newspapers across the West Coast as the 'The Bearded Bank Bandit'. After a failed escape attempt during a prison riot in which six prison officers were killed, Grant was transferred to Alcatraz where he died of blood poisoning. He was one bad criminal.*"

Zixin frowned. "Hard to think he did any painting."

"But if he did, then where are they now?" said Nat.

The door opened and Aunt Vera came in. She was dressed, not in her usual Shan-xi glamour but in a simple black jumper and trousers. Her mushroom hair was slicked back into a pony tail and she wasn't wearing the usual mask of make-up. She looked younger by about a hundred years.

"*Well, hello!*" said the goat, admiringly.

Chapter Twenty-Eight
AUNT VERA

Aunt Vera sat down on the edge of the coffee table, next to the goat. Nat couldn't smell the usual waft of stinky perfume.

"Has someone died, Mummy?" said Henry.

Nat gulped. Maybe it was Uncle Fergal, or even Prissy...

"No one's died, Henry, just my old self. I heard you come in and get my FastPad, Natalie, and I followed you. I've been listening and watching everything from behind that door."

Nat's mind raced through recent events – the operation on the dining table, Zixin and Henry, the films and photos from Alcatraz.

"*You some kinda spy?*" said the goat.

Aunt Vera shook her head. "No, but I am a greedy, shallow woman. Your words hit hard, Natalie: '*If she ever comes out of her room again, tell her I said she should go shopping, spend as much money as she likes, but just keep out of my way.*'"

Nat squirmed. She'd meant what she'd said, every single word, but hearing them come from her aunt's mouth was like fingernails scraping down the side of the *Junko*.

"And Henry, I heard you say all those things about me when you were talking with Zixin. Am I that bad a person?"

Henry turned bright red. He opened and closed his mouth, like a fish out of water. Nothing came out.

"Yes, you are," said Nat, coming to his aid. She had no idea what he'd said, but she could guess that it wasn't at all pleasant. "You are that bad, which is why we say all these things behind your back, because you don't like being told to your face."

Aunt Vera took a sharp intake of breath. Nat got ready for her to totally lose it and explode, right back to her old self. Instead…

"If the Alcatraz visitor centre operates like any other gallery then they won't have all the paintings out at once. They'll have an archive, where the rest of the collection will be stored so they can rotate paintings and keep the exhibition fresh. Also, since the paintings were done by prisoners they are most likely catalogued by their prisoner number rather than their proper name. The best way to find out would be to go there."

Nat's jaw dropped. She wasn't expecting that. Aunt Vera was now smiling, which was even weirder.

"See? I do know some useful things. I worked at the Pignon-Pie Art Gallery before I met Fergal, but when we got married he said he didn't want me working any more. I should never have listened to him."

The goat started to tap dance on the table. *"You're one smart cookie. Let's scram and get this sorted!"*

Zixin was up on his feet.

"I'm in. Thanks, Vera. You know some good stuff. The sooner we check it out the better. You ready, Nat?"

She turned to her shoulder where Fizz was normally perched, half-expecting him to be there. The second she saw it empty her heart sank. Where was he? And even worse, what if Lang Liu had done something to him?

"While you go to Alcatraz," said Vera, "Henry and I will take a trip to Chinatown to see what we can discover about this Hong man. We might even find Fizz."

Nat had a sudden urge to hug her aunt but before she did anything so *un-ku* she was saved by the goat who leapt off the table and used its horns to push her towards the door.

"Give me five to brief Vera on Hong's gaff, and I'll meet you at the elevator," shouted Zixin, as Nat headed out into the hall.

Chapter Twenty-Nine
RAY'S ROCKETS

Nat rode the Slider down the hill with Zixin and the goat sat on the back. It was even slower with all of them on board, and they kept being overtaken. Now she wished they'd taken a GrooveCab. She would have preferred the crazy music to this tortoise pace. And they'd be at the Rocketboat rental place by now.

The goat kept shouting "howdy" to anyone dressed in the Goldrush fashion, and if it wasn't doing that it was firing questions at Zixin about his grandad. She couldn't properly hear what was being said though because the street they were on had cable cars clunking and clanking along their tracks.

When they finally pulled up at "Ray's Rockets" she felt like she'd wasted a day just getting there, and they didn't have that kind of time. Lang Liu might already have found Gan Jiang.

"How much is it for you to take us out there and then wait for us at the jetty?" she said to the guy at the boat-rental desk.

"Well how long will you be?"

She shrugged. "I don't know. An hour, all day, it depends."

The guy checked his FastPad. "Well, it's a busy day for us."

"I've got dosh," said Zixin, getting out the envelope from inside his jacket.

The guy's eyes lit up when he saw the stack of twenty-dollar bills bulging out.

"I'll take you myself for a thousand," he said.

"Deal. We go right now, though, and you wait at the jetty until we're ready to come back."

Minutes later they were cutting through a thick bank of fog, rocketing across the choppy, indigo waters towards Alcatraz Island. Nat zipped up her Slider jacket as high as it would go to try and stop the cold seeping in.

The island soon came looming up before them, looking like some haunted castle in a ghost story. Lang Liu was there somewhere. She half expected him to come swooping out of the fog.

"*Welcome to Alcatraz,*" said an android ranger, giving her a hand up on to the jetty.

The goat leapt out next to her.

"*Well, well, some places never change. This looks exactly like it did when I was last here. Follow me.*"

It trotted off towards the visitor centre where a queue of people were waiting to get inside.

"*VIPs coming through,*" it said, leading her and Zixin to the front.

It had its head down, horns at the ready, so people moved out of their way, fast. Nat kept her head down and followed it inside.

They came out into a large warehouse-sized room, which housed the exhibition. There were arrows guiding the crowds through in a one-way only direction, so even the goat had to shuffle along until they came to the art gallery.

It ducked under a rope barrier and head-butted a door open marked "*Staff Only*". Nat and Zixin slipped through and they came out into the stairway that they'd seen on the map earlier. Keeping to the plan they headed down the stairs to a set of fire doors.

"*Showtime?*" said the goat.

Nat nodded. It lowered its horns and pushed the doors open. Inside lay a windowless, strip-lighted room, where a woman in a brown ranger uniform was sitting at a desk piled high with old paper folders.

"Well, hey there, folks! It's not often I get company

down here. What can I do you for?" she said, looking at them over the top of her glasses.

"Hello. We're on an overseas school visit from London," said Nat, ready to get going with her rehearsed speech.

They'd agreed she'd lead, the goat would keep quiet, and Zixin would back her up.

"You've come all the way from London, England?" said the woman, leaning her elbows on the files.

"Yes, London, England. We're from Boxbury School and we've got to do a special scholarship project while we're here. Zixin and I are doing research on an old prisoner of Alcatraz. His name was Barbury Grant. We've read all the information upstairs, but a ranger said he was an artist too, and that we should come down and ask you for more information."

The woman sucked the air slowly into her mouth until her cheeks bulged out hamster-style. She sat back in her chair and clasped her hands around the back of her head. "Well now, you've sure picked yourselves a character there. That was one complex kinda guy. Ruthless bank robber on the outside. They say he killed over thirty people. But on the inside, my oh my, there was a tortured creative soul."

She slapped her hand on the desk so loudly they

all jumped. She scraped back her chair and got to her feet.

"Scholarship, you say?"

"Yeah, we've got to make a mega presentation to take back to show the scholarship committee at school. So any help you can give us would be wicked," said Zixin.

The ranger pulled a large bunch of keys out of a desk drawer.

"I like the way you're both so interested in furthering your education. Aren't many students these days as fired up like I can see you two are. You remind me of me when I was your age. A thirst for knowledge. Well, you've come to the right place. Follow me."

Chapter Thirty
A DARK DISCOVERY

The ranger unlocked a steel door on the other side of the room. They followed her into a massive underground storage warehouse. It smelled of stale sea air, like the dive-suit locker on the *Junko*. Floor-to-ceiling metal racks stood in long rows stacked with boxes and sealed plastic bags. Each aisle was lit by dim, overhead lamps.

"We do it by prisoner number. Here we are. Prisoner B315: Mr Barbury Grant," she said, stopping halfway down a row.

The ranger pulled out a long box from one of the shelves and opened the lid. Inside was a side-stacked pile of small canvases. She lifted the first one out. Chills ran down Nat's spine. Tiger's teeth, this was it! The painting of the bridge.

"So, as you see, he was an oil painter. All his paintings were done in oil. Now, what do you notice about this picture?"

She unclipped a torch from her belt and lit the

painting as if they were in some fancy gallery. Zixin and Nat leaned in closer.

"The colours are really dark," said Nat.

The woman laughed. "You sure are scholarship kids because you are absolutely right! Grant only painted in shades of indigo. It's like he was obsessed. Here."

She put the painting back in the box and lifted out the next one. Nat wondered if her mind was playing tricks. It was exactly the same scene as the last one. She tried to count up how many canvases there were. If they were all of the bridge, then how long would it take to work out which one was under MacDuff's pillow in the photo?

"Another thing about Grant you should know," continued the ranger, "is that for every week he was in Alcatraz he painted the same picture of the Golden Gate Bridge."

"How many weeks was he here for?" asked Zixin.

The woman waved her hand at a shelf stacked high with boxes.

"One hundred and eighty four. Then he died in his cell. Blood poisoning, they said, but some people think it might have been more sinister than that."

"Would it be all right if we looked at them all?" said Nat.

The woman grinned and popped some gum in her mouth. "Well, you two are the most studious kids I've met in a long while! I've got work to do but if you'd like you can stay and go through the boxes. I can't let you take them out of here, though, them's the rules."

"Wicked, thanks," said Zixin.

"You can use my torch," she said, passing it to Nat. "Come on out when you're done. I'll be at my desk."

The ranger walked off, her brown boots clomping along the concrete floor. The goat activated its torch eyes.

"Can I talk now?" it said.

"Go ahead," said Nat, while Zixin reached up and lifted another box from the shelf.

"Nice work. You've found out stuff me and your grandad never did on all our trips here."

Zixin lifted the lid and pulled a canvas out. "You'd think he might have branched out and painted something else, just for a change."

Nat picked out the next in her box. The bridge was dark, almost black. The sky was a stormy mix of mottled indigo blues, from light to dark. A layer of blue fog was coming in from the ocean. The waters below seemed almost violet. The oil was thick, giving it a 3D effect. She liked the painting, even if it had been painted by a cold-blooded criminal. It drew you into its darkness.

"He was in the cell next to MacDuff so I guess it was the only view he had. I think we should lay them all out on the floor," she said, putting it down on the concrete. "Then we can do a sort of spot-the-difference."

Zixin groaned. "A one hundred and eighty-four spot the difference."

"*I can help out with that. Let's do it!*" said the goat.

They hauled out all the boxes and lined up the paintings until the floor of the aisle looked like it had been tiled.

"*I'll take it from the top. You guys search, too,*" said the goat, switching its eyes from torch to scan mode.

Nat used the torch that the woman had lent her and started from the bottom, while Zixin joined the goat.

The goat moved fast, uploading each painting in a second. It had tracked halfway down while Nat had only checked out a couple. She was about to move on to the third painting when something in the swirling, pale, indigo fog caught her eye. She moved the torch closer to where the brushstrokes of fog curled under the bridge.

"Hey, check this out."

The goat and Zixin came to where she was kneeling.

"Look," she said, directing the torch beam on to one of the feet of the bridge's two towers.

Under the veil of fog was a pencil outline drawing of a mermaid. She was upside down, tail out of the water, head below the surface. Her right arm was fully extended. In her hand she grasped a sword, which was pointing to the depths below. The goat let out a long whistle.

"Nice work, Natalie. The sword's down there in the land of Great White Sharks."

Chapter Thirty-One
TUK TUK

It was Lang Liu who spotted them hightailing off back to the city in a Rocketboat. He and Scorta were up at the main cell block. Scorta was busy digging up MacDuff's cell floor with its steel claws, while he'd perched up on the barred windows.

From where he was he had a bird's eye view of the jetty below, and he'd seen Zixin and the girl come running out of the visitor centre with some small silver robot on four legs.

"Leave that, we're going now," he said.

He took off, flying out into the cellblock. Scorta came chasing after him. They headed outside, down the hill to the VIP mooring zone.

"Where's my bloody Rocketboat?" he roared.

"*On its way,*" said Scorta.

Lang Liu flapped up into the air. "I'm going after them. Let me know when you get to shore."

The city was further away than he thought. The wind was up too, so he had to flap harder. He hadn't done this sort of exercise in many years, but he didn't care. The way those kids had bolted out of the visitor centre and hopped on a Rocketboat he just knew they'd found out something to do with the missing sword. So the sooner he got to them, the sooner he'd do the trade. A sword for Fizz, a sword for Vesperetta, that was the perfect symmetry of the deal.

He was a short distance from shore when he spotted them getting into a GrooveCab. His arms ached from being flapped up and down by the robotic wings. His breath was short, but all that would be solved when he united Mo Ye and Gan Jiang. He'd become a super-human, a living hybrid.

The GrooveCab took a right, along the Embarcadero, so Lang Liu pitched right, tracking them.

Where were they going? And where was Scorta when he needed it?

An old tuk tuk motorbike sat parked at a quay further up. The driver was laid back in his seat, taking a nap. Lang Liu used the last of his energy to swoop down. His claws clanged on to the metal handlebars. The driver opened his eyes, took one look at the man's head on an eagle body, freaked out and fell sideways on to the ground.

"Don't hurt me, man! Please don't eat me!" he

screamed, squeezing his eyes closed, protecting his head with his hands.

"Idiot. Of course I'm not going to eat you! I just need a ride. I'll pay you well if you move fast."

Lang Liu hopped into the back seat. The guy scrambled to his feet.

"Your head looks freakily way more real than a normal android man, and the bird body... What's with the mix?"

The driver was trembling from head to toe. Lang Liu raised an eyebrow.

"Drive, just drive. No questions and I'll pay you five hundred bucks if you can follow that cab over there all the way to its destination."

The driver gulped.

"Five hundred?"

"Yes, it's done. Now get going before it gets away!"

The driver checked his Wrister. His fare counter read "*Fare paid $500.*"

He jumped into the driver's seat, let off the brakes, and twisted the throttle. A blue plume of old fries fuel farted out of the exhaust, and the bike lurched forward with a deafening roar.

The ride was bumpy and deafening. The guy was a crazy driver. He weaved in and out of traffic using both the vehicle and Slider lanes. People honked their horns, shook their fists, but the five hundred dollars had done the trick, they were hot on the trail.

"*Scorta here. We've landed at RocketBoat Rentals,*" squeaked the guinea-lion into his nano-dot earpiece.

"Put your tracer on and follow me," said Lang Liu.

Up ahead, the GrooveCab was already on the Golden Gate Bridge, moving at speed.

"The twenty-dollar bridge fee is additional to the five-hundred," shouted the driver.

Lang Liu sighed. Typical. You gave somebody a generous fee for a menial job and then they started to mess with you. The greedy side surfaced. They felt empowered that they'd found a rich sucker. "Pull over. Pull over now!" he shouted.

"What? I can't, we're on the bridge," shouted the driver over the din of the traffic.

Lang Liu clamped a claw on to the driver's back.

"Pull over now!"

The driver screamed and swerved across two lanes. The tuk tuk mounted the sidewalk, scattering tourists like a fox among chickens. Lang Liu took off, out of the passenger seat, up into the fog. If there hadn't been so many tourists he'd have taken the driver with him and dropped him off the bridge into the waters below.

INDIGO ISLAND

He tracked the GrooveCab all the way to the "Sail'n'Dip'n'Dive" rental store in Sausalito.

Not wanting to be spotted, he landed in a nearby palm tree, where he came eye to eye with a mockingbird. It squawked in terror and fled its nest.

He waited, keeping an eye on the door of the store. The whole perching thing was getting on his nerves. In Hong Kong he had a red velvet couch, where he'd spread his wings and lounge back. A few minutes later Scorta squeaked into his earpiece.

"*We're here.*"

He spotted them below, padding around the base of the tree.

"Lay low. You see that cafe on the opposite side of the road? Go and wait there, behind that red truck."

"*Yes, boss.*"

An hour later the girl and Zixin emerged. The silver, four-legged thing was a miniature goat. He guessed it was some sort of hotel bot that they'd got on loan.

Both the girl and Zixin were wearing cold-water skins with dive packs strapped to their backs. A saleswoman was taking them out to the water's edge to where a couple of kite boards were tethered up. Lang Liu angled his sound catcher towards them in time to pick up what she said next.

"Have fun, y'all. Remember to keep to the safe areas I showed you on the map. Don't go beyond the green zone and be back by five."

Chapter Thirty-Two
GAN JIANG

The last time Nat had gone kite-surfing was with Jamuka when they were living in Hong Kong. They'd sailed out to Lama Island where the water had been so clear you could see the rainbow fish below, and above the skies were a clear blue. The wind had filled their kites and blown them along the shore until they'd reached a golden cove where they'd landed and eaten a delicious picnic.

This trip was nothing like that one. The moment they launched off the shore into the Bay, the wind picked up. Nat leaned back on the board to counteract the pull of her harness from the orange kite above. She gripped on to the bar and felt its raw power as the board flew across the water at high speed.

Freezing water was seeping through the soles of her wetsuit boots, and she was trying not to think of what might be swimming around in the grey swell below.

"Hey, this is some kinda crazy ride!" shouted the

goat, from where it was zipped into her backpack.

She turned to check on Zixin. He was down in the water again. She flipped the kite and headed back to him.

"You OK?" she shouted.

He gave her the thumbs up. "Keep going. I'll catch you up!"

Nat set off again towards the far tower of the bridge, where the upside-down mermaid had been in the painting. The wind kept gusting and changing direction, while the water was getting darker and choppier. She could feel the tide pulling her out to sea. Rat's tails, she'd been stupid to think they could just zip out to the tower, do a quick dive to get Gan Jiang, and be back by five. Even the goat had retreated into the backpack and zipped itself inside.

An image of Fizz flashed through her mind. He was dressed in the parrot suit, wings slumped, his snout masked by a beak. *Zoinks*, that was the fuel she needed. She leaned back further on her board, the kite pulled harder, straining the harness and trying to wrench her arms from their sockets, but she tightened her grip. She'd got nothing to lose except herself, and she'd rather die trying to get Fizz back than never have him with her again.

She caught a wave and launched up into the air. The fog lifted and she could clearly see the metal struts of the tower only a short distance away. She landed on the water, flipped the kite, and came sweeping around in a wide arc towards the platform.

A wave was just cresting, so she took her chance and aimed for it. The board hit it, lifted and she landed on the concrete. She quickly pulled her kite in and stood there, catching her breath, staring up at the giant iron tower. The howling wind was now mixed with the drone and rumble of bridge traffic overhead.

"Wicked!" said Zixin, landing close by. "Southend-on-Sea's got nothing on this!"

"Great work getting here," said the goat, leaping out of the backpack that Nat had dropped on the ground.

"It took way longer than I thought. We've not much time before dark."

She reached into the pack and pulled out a regulator, mask, flippers, and gloves. The dive uniform. Some kids had toys growing up, she'd had diving equipment.

She started to put it on while the goat gave them a run down of the bridge statistics – its size, age, how long it took to build, and how many great white sharks had probably passed underneath it.

While it talked, the Bay was whipping up into white

caps and the fog was once again rolling in. Nat pulled on her mask, checked her regulator and turned to where Zixin sat, fiddling with his dive tank.

"Wait for me here. I'm going to check it out."

He shook his head. "No way. I let you do that last time. I'll be ready in a sec."

She was no longer listening though, because she could feel something begin to pull her to the edge, like a giant magnet. Before she could stop it she fell over and plunged down into the water. The cold was intense. She could feel her heart speed up, then slow, as she was pulled downwards, deeper and deeper into the dark abyss.

She was diving too fast, she wouldn't be able to regulate. She started to breathe faster, sucking in oxygen from her tank.

Then, as quickly as the pull had started, it stopped, leaving her suspended in the underwater gloom. In front of her she could see the concrete wall of the tower covered in thick layers of seaweed and barnacles. Something was pulsing out a faint light underneath.

She reached out and started to clear off the seaweed. It was tricky in the thick, rented gloves so she removed one to get a better grip. As she swept the seaweed to one side her fingers brushed the glowing object.

INDIGO ISLAND

There was a sudden explosion of electric blue light. It lit the sea bed like a snapshot. She saw a humpback whale passing by in the distance, looking like some giant submarine. A rusty old Cadillac lay on the ocean floor below, and a shoal of fish was making its way towards the city. Something slapped into the palm of her hand with such force that she screamed in pain. If she'd been above water they'd have heard her from up on the bridge.

She looked down to find her fingers wrapped around a metal hilt. She hadn't found Gan Jiang, it had found her.

As quickly as the light came, it vanished, and she was plunged into darkness. She flippered upwards, her arm dragging with the weight of the sword.

She broke the surface, pulled out her regulator and took deep breaths of salty air. The fog was now swirling around her in a thick soup. She'd no idea which way the bridge lay, or the city.

"Zixin!" she shouted, but there was no reply.

She didn't know which way to swim.

"Anyone there?"

There was a loud squawk. An enormous pair of claws came swooping down out of the fog. They grabbed her shoulders, the talons digging into her wet suit, and dragged her up and out of the water.

"No! Let me go!" she screamed, seeing Lang Liu's head.

She tried to lift her arm and swipe him with the sword, but he dug his talons in deeper, pinning her shoulder.

He pulled them up high, flapping through the fog until he came to land, dropping her on to the ground.

"Give it to me," he said, grabbing at the sword with his talons.

He pulled but she hung on. He pulled again. He took his talons and tried to scrape her fingers off its hilt, but it was as if they were glued on.

"Give me the sword!" he roared.

"No!" she cried. "Not until you give me Fizz back!"

He jumped on her chest, leaning his head in towards her.

"Want your little dragon that much?"

She tried to arch her back enough to jump up, but he was too heavy.

"Bring me Fizz and I will give you Gan Jiang."

He spread his wings and took off, swooping over to once again grasp the sword in his talons. He lifted it, but Nat came with it. Pain shot through her as it wrenched her arm. It was so intense she had to let go, but when she tried to release her fingers from the hilt, she couldn't.

"Stop! It's attached to my skin, I can't let it go!"

Lang Liu dropped the sword. She fell on to the ground with such force that she blacked out.

Chapter Thirty-Three
ESCAPE FROM ALCATRAZ

Nat opened her eyes. She was lying on a thin, striped mattress that smelled damp and mouldy. Above, an old bare lightbulb hung from a faded green ceiling. The paint was cracked and peeling. She moved her head to one side to find a row of rusty bars. No, she couldn't be... She was back on Alcatraz in a cell.

Lang Liu was standing on the other side of the bars, staring at her with his bloodshot eyes. She opened her mouth to call for help. Nothing came out but a raspy whisper. She could feel the cold metal hilt of Gan Jiang in her palm. Fizz, if only she had Fizz...

She tried to move her feet but they'd been tied down with rope.

"Don't bother trying to escape," said Lang Liu. "We're in a closed off area here. Save your screams, girl. No one will hear you."

"Please let me go," she rasped. "You can have the sword. Fizz will know how to make it leave my hand. If you bring Fizz, he'll do it."

"*Reporting in for duty.*"

The shaggy pig-lion appeared at Lang Liu's side.

"About time, you good-for-nothing bot. Now make yourself useful, go in there and rip the sword off her."

Rip?

"No! Please, no! Fizz knows how to get the sword off me. Please!"

She kicked her feet trying to free them from the rope as the pig-lion pulled back the cell door.

It pinned her with a massive paw and opened its mouth to reveal a set of Samurai-sharp teeth.

"Nooo!" Nat screamed, finding her voice, trying to wriggle free. "Let me go!"

A loud bleating sound echoed through the cell. A blur of silver came flying through the air, straight into pig-lion, knocking it off her with such force that it flew through the open cell door on to the gangway.

The pig-lion let out a ferocious roar and came back up on to its haunches, but the goat lowered its horns and charged.

There was a flash and crackle of electricity as its horns pierced the pig-lion's fur. The goat's eyes had turned ruby red and it started blasting it with electric shocks. The pig-lion burst into flames, triggering the cellblock fire alarm.

"Give me that sword!" screamed Lang Liu, flying at Nat, his talons digging into her hand.

She saw her chance. She rolled towards him, whipping her left leg so fast in a tiger-kick that it tore through the rope and caught him on the side of his head, knocking him sideways.

She didn't hesitate. She lifted the sword and with one swift downwards stroke of the blade she pierced his outstretched wing, pinning him to the ground. He let out a blood-curdling scream, rolling from side to side, trying to break free.

Zixin came sprinting in, raised an arm and chopped his grandad at the neck, which knocked him out.

"*Quick, we gotta go. The rangers will be here any moment,*" said the goat.

Zixin helped Nat free her other foot from the rope, and then used it to lasso around his grandad's bird-body.

"I'll carry him," he said.

She pulled the sword out of Lang Liu's wing so that Zixin could fold it in. He then wound the rope around his eagle body like a cotton reel and hefted him on to his shoulder.

"*Zoula!*" said Nat, running out of the cell, dodging

around the bonfire of fake fur and robot pieces that was once the pig-lion.

The thundering sound of footsteps came echoing up from the cellblock floor below.

"*Follow me*," said the goat, galloping off along the gangway.

They sprinted after it, around a corner, and came to the end. There were no stairs, only metal barrier rails. The shouts of the rangers were getting louder.

"Jump on my shoulder," said Nat.

The goat leapt up. She lifted a leg over the rails. It was a steep drop down to the cellblock floor.

"Ninja jump," she said to Zixin. "I'll go first."

She didn't wait for him to reply. She scrambled down the railings until there was nothing else left to hang off. Then she let go, but as she did she kicked out, propelling herself over to the cellblock wall. The moment her foot touched it she sprang off, coming to land in a crouching tiger position on the ground.

"*Smooth moves,*" said the goat, hopping off on to the floor.

She stood up and looked up. Zixin wasn't there.

"Zix…"

But before she could finish he came flying over the railing. He'd unraveled the rope from around his grandad, stretched the eagle bot wings to full span, and was headed her way, hanging on to the eagle talons.

He came gliding to the ground, snapped the wings back in and lassoed the rope around once more. Lang Liu's eyes were still shut.

"He's still out, let's move it," said Zixin.

The goat head-butted open a rusting side door and they came out into the foggy darkness of night on Alcatraz.

"Follow me," said the goat, leading them down a steep, rocky path to the water's edge.

The silhouette of a Rocketboat was bobbing on the water, just off-shore. The goat let out a shrill whistle and she heard the engines fire up.

It was the guy from earlier. He pulled in close enough for them to jump onboard.

"Wow, I'm not gonna mess with you," he said, seeing the sword in Nat's hand.

"And what is that thing?" he said, seeing Lang Liu.

"You don't want to know. I've paid you enough, so no more questions. Just get us back fast," said Zixin.

The guy mock-saluted and grabbed the wheel.

"Hang on tight. I'm going to take us up to full throttle."

The Rocketboat began to fly across the water. Nat

rested the sword tip on the deck and gripped on to the seat handles. The moment they were back on shore she'd wake up Lang Liu and force him to give her Fizz back.

"Hey, cut the speed, hang a left. We've got company, friend not foe!" shouted the goat.

The guy slowed the engines and turned the boat. A fog horn sounded close by. Nat stood up. She could see a pattern of pale blue lights glowing in the gloom. Her heart started to beat faster. The prow of a large ocean-going vessel appeared.

"Looks like some ancient pirate ship," said the guy.

Nat had never been so pleased to see the *Junko* in all her life.

Chapter Thirty-Four
THE JUNKO

Nat climbed up the ladder on to the deck of the *Junko*. She ran over the wooden planks to the upper deck to where Ah Ping was at the wheel, dressed in Jamuka's old Mongolian coat and fur hat. She threw her one free arm around her, and hugged her close.

"*Zoinks*, you made it! How did you find us?"

Ah Ping smiled.

"Long trip. I talk with Henry, big happenings. You get the sword!"

Nat held up Gan Jiang. Her arm felt like it was going to drop off having to haul it around. Maybe it'd never come off. Maybe she was stuck with it forever. Ah Ping looked it up and down.

"Look same as Mo Ye."

There was a loud thud on deck as Zixin landed Lang Liu like a big fish.

"*Hey captain, at your service,*" said the goat, bombing up the steps and coming to a screeching halt at Ah Ping's feet.

Ah Ping reached down and touched one of its horns. "Goat is lucky. I was born in year of goat."

The goat started to tap dance, but stopped.

"Incoming update from NutNut. We must intercept them at The St Francis Yacht Club."

Ah Ping switched the *Junko* to the MaxEdge auto pilot.

"No sails. We motor there," she said, leaving the wheel. "That bird man?"

She was pointing to the rolled up Lang Liu on the main deck. His eyes were open and he was groaning, while Zixin adjusted the ropes.

"Yes, and I need to know where he's got Fizz."

"I talk to him," said Ah Ping, heading down with the goat hot on her heels.

Nat watched her crouch down and start talking fast and furious at Lang Liu in Cantonese. She could hear words like "greedy pig" and "Kowloon criminal" coming from Ah Ping.

She stopped listening because the hilt of the sword was beginning to get really hot in her palm. Her fingers went from tingling to burning. She tried to tug her hand away, but it was useless. Instead the sword started glowing and pulling her towards the main hatch.

The others didn't notice as she was dragged down below deck. Gan Jiang was on a mission and she could guess where to.

She had to take the stairs two at a time as it pulled her towards her parents' old cabin. As soon as they reached the door Gan Jiang jabbed it open and sprang from her hand like an arrow being shot from a bow. It flew through the air, dropped down to the dragon-patterned silk rug, and whisked it to one side as if it was drawing back a curtain.

Quick as a flash it hooked the tip of its blade through the brass handle that was set into the floor, and ripped open the secret locker.

A shaft of moonlight shot up and out of the silver casing below, and the Mo Ye sword came flying out. Nat ducked as it hurtled around the room. There was a deafening clash of metal as the two swords reunited. Sparks came exploding out, showering down. She covered her eyes to shield them from the glare. All the stories of the swords and what they might do came tumbling through her head – ultimate power, everlasting youth, the power to bring things to life, to lengthen life…

Something heavy clattered into the locker. Silence fell. Nat peeped through her fingers. The room had gone dark. She reached over and switched on the bedside lamp. Nothing in the cabin was out of place except the rug. The blue-silk blind covering the porthole was down. The double bed was neatly made up with white linen sheets.

She stepped across to the edge of the locker and peered inside. Instead of two swords there was now just one. Gan Jiang and Mo Ye had forged together to form a single, large broadsword. The metal shone bright gold as if someone had just polished it. At the top of the blade, near the hilt, there was a perfect heart-shaped hole.

So this was it? She reached in and touched the hilt. It was cold. It didn't move. Maybe this was the end, Mo Ye and Gan Jiang had finally found each other and love was restored. All of those people who had been searching for this... And then there were those who'd died because of it, like Jamuka...

"Nat! Where are you?"

Henry. She could hear his footsteps coming down the stairs. She quickly closed the locker and whipped the rug back in place. Until they'd dealt with Lang Liu she'd keep this a secret.

"Here," she said, walking out into the corridor.

Henry turned and came running towards her. His

hair was on end and his face was red.

"We've got Hong. Mummy and I were watching his shop. It was all locked up to start with, but then Hong came back. He unlocked the door and went inside so we followed him and I showed Mummy my flying kick. I got Hong on the back of his head. He fell down, then Mummy bashed him with her shoe. We tied him up with lots of bandages that we'd bought from the chemists and then Mummy interrogated him. She was scary. She got him to admit that he knew where Fizz and Vesperetta were so we stuffed him in a Grooverider and brought him here."

Fizz. That was all she wanted – to have her dragon back. Henry was tugging her arm.

"Come on, he's up on deck with the horrid bird man."

They came out of the main hatch. Hong and Lang Liu were tied up around the main mast. Aunt Vera was shouting at Hong; Ah Ping and Zixin were doing the same at Lang Liu.

"STOP!" yelled Nat.

They all turned to her. She held up both hands into the air.

"Where's Gan Jiang?" said Lang Liu.

"It's reunited with Mo Ye. There is no ultimate

power in them. They're just swords."

"Show me."

Fury and rage came bubbling up inside her. She ran at Lang Liu and one-inch punched him in the face. He roared in pain and anger.

"Show me? You don't get that privilege, you foul bird man. Look at your life, everything you've done, how you've used your grandson to get what you want. And what's it all come to? NOTHING! All you do is destroy people's lives, LIKE MINE! And I'm NOT GOING TO LET YOU DO THAT ANYMORE!"

She pulled back her fist ready to punch him again, but Ah Ping's hand shot out and blocked her.

"Better way than this," she said.

"*You sure?*" said the goat. "*I'd suggest one more round so he tells us where Fizz and Vesperetta are.*"

Zixin stepped in front of his grandad. He reached in between the ropes to where his neck met with the eagle feathers and slipped his hand around the back. Lang Liu squealed.

"Don't do something you'll regret!"

There was a click and a rushing of air like a deflating balloon. The eagle body opened up like a clam, breaking the ropes. Inside lay Lang Liu's shrivelled body wearing a shiny lime-green tracksuit. Zixin grabbed him and hauled him out on to the deck.

"We're staying here until you tell us where you've hidden Fizz and Vesperetta."

"Hey!"

The goat took off charging across the deck. No one had noticed that Hong was making a getaway. He didn't get far though because the goat lowered its horns and charged right at Hong's bottom.

"Yeoooooowwwww!" cried Hong, as he was tossed up into the night sky.

He landed back right next to Lang Liu.

Chapter Thirty-Five
RESCUE

The goat led the way with its eyes in torch mode, down the stairs into Hong's basement. Nat and Zixin found the safe in the far corner, next to the furnace, exactly where Hong had described.

The goat read out the code that Lang Liu had finally given them, and Nat keyed it into the digital reader. The locks ratcheted back and the door sprang open.

Her heart was thumping, her hands were shaking as she reached inside and pulled out a long metal box. She had no idea what to expect. What if Fizz was in pieces? What if Lang Liu had removed his brain?

Zixin snapped the latches open. Her hand flew to her mouth, her stomach lurched as he lifted the lid. She squeezed her eyes shut.

"It's safe to look," said Zixin.

The goat had spotlit the inside of the box. She peered inside. Fizz and Vesperetta were lying side by side. Each one was attached by Spiderwire to a mini power-pack.

"I bet he'd got them charging so they could join his army," said Zixin, lifting Vesperetta out.

She reached in and lifted out her little dragon. She placed her finger on the underside of his wing.

His eyes snapped open. The second he saw her they flashed from green to purple. He ruffled his scales.

"*You came to my rescue,*" he said.

She smiled. "It took me a while, with a little help from our friends."

"*Fizz! Great to have you back bro!*" said the goat, leaping into the air and spinning around.

"*You escaped the mansion?*"

"*Sure did, I'm a free goat!*"

Fizz's head turned to where Zixin was standing with Vesperetta wrapped around his neck. Her snake head was leaning in close to his ear. She was whispering something that was making him smile.

"*What's she doing here?*" he said, snorting out a plume of smoke.

"Long story. First let's get out of here."

They headed out of Hong's and into a waiting GrooveCab. By the time they reached the yacht club they'd got both robots up to speed on what had gone down in their absence.

Dawn was breaking when they arrived at the quay.

INDIGO ISLAND

The fog had cleared, and the sun was rising into a blue sky. Henry was waiting for them up on the *Junko's* deck. The second he saw them he came running down the gangplank.

"You've got them back! Hooray! Mummy and Ah Ping are down in the galley having coffee. Hong and bird man are locked in the storage room. Philippe's on the SPIN jet now. He says he'll be here tonight to sort them out. Mummy said we can all have pancakes delivered but I've waited until you came back to find out what kind you want."

All Nat wanted to do was get out of the wet suit, put on an old Slider t-shirt and shorts, collapse on deck and chill out with Fizz.

"*Ku*. Blueberry for me, please. I'll be back in a sec. Just need to change."

She headed through the main hatch. Laughter and loud chatter were coming out of the open galley door. That was a first for her aunt and Ah Ping. She passed by and headed into the corridor.

"*I feel out of sorts,*" said Fizz, from where he was perched on her shoulders. "*Something's not right.*"

He let out a loud burp and started shaking. Something came loose inside him and began to rattle like a pebble in a jar. Smoke started billowing out of his snout. Nat reached up but before she could grab him he took off, flying up the corridor.

"Fizz!" she shouted, chasing after him.

Vile bird man must have done something to him.

He stopped at her parents' cabin door, swooped down, turned the handle and flew inside. Nat sprinted in after him. The rug that had covered the floor was pulled back. The locker was open and the sword was out, standing on end, its tip balanced on a floorboard.

Fizz had landed next to it. His whole body was now juddering and convulsing. He opened his snout and let out a blast of flames.

She dived down to scoop him up but just as she did a fireball came flying out of his mouth, his eyes snapped shut, and he fell backwards on to the floor. A wisp of smoke came curling out of his nostrils.

"Fizz?"

She picked him up and cradled him in her palms. He didn't move. Out of the corner of her eye she caught sight of a red glow. She turned, blinked, not quite believing what she was seeing. The fireball had gone and in its place lay a heart-shaped ruby.

There was a blinding flash. She was hurled back against the cabin wall. The sword came crashing to the floor next to her. *Zoinks!* The ruby had fitted itself into the heart-shaped hole in the blade like a Cinderella slipper.

But now her hand was empty. Where was Fizz? She scrambled on to her hands and knees. He was nowhere to be seen.

"Fizz?"

She crawled across to the locker and looked over the edge. He was lying inside on his back, talons in the air. She reached in and picked him up.

He opened his eyes. She gulped. Instead of their usual green colour they had turned a bright sky blue. He sat up and stretched out his wings.

"Wow, I can feel my body!"

His voice was new, lower and less like a robot.

He wriggled his talons, moved his head from side to side, and shook his wings like a dog throwing off the rain.

"I can feel everything, Nat!"

He took off, flying round and round the cabin.

"I can smell jasmine!" he shouted.

She frowned. "What's happened to you?"

He swooped down, took hold of her hand in his talons and placed it on the scales on his chest. Instead of the familiar feel of his inner mechanisms whirring and ratcheting she felt a steady heartbeat. Impossible.

"Open your snout," she said.

He leaned his head back and opened up. She peered inside expecting to see the robotic pieces and parts. In their place was a pink throat. His stomach made a loud gurgling sound.

"I'm hungry. Really hungry. I need real food."

She looked from him to the sword. Had it brought him to life?

"How did that ruby get inside you?"

He shrugged. "No idea. I don't need it anymore, though, I've got my own heart."

He flew up on to her shoulder, and wrapped his wings around her neck.

"I love you, Natalie Walker, and I will always be your dragon."

Chapter Thirty-Six
FIZZ

Nat sat on the deck of the *Junko* watching the Golden Gate bridge draw closer. It had been two weeks since she had last been out here on the water. She shivered at the thought of how she had kite-surfed to the south tower in the fog to find the sword, and how the bird man had swooped down and grabbed her. It felt much longer ago, somewhere in the dim and distant past.

Lang Liu was long gone now. Philippe had arrived in the V-Styler jet, picked him up and taken him to SPIN headquarters in Hong Kong. Once there he had been forced to transfer over his hybrid robot company, Batcan, to Zixin. After it was confirmed that Zixin was the sole owner, the V-Styler had transported Lang Liu to a clinic far away in the mountains in China. He wouldn't be coming out again for a very long time.

His nasty sidekick, Hong, had promised to never make contact with Lang Liu ever again, and had been allowed to go back to his shop. To keep an eye on him, Philippe had sent a SPIN bug bot to monitor him at all times.

Today was one hundred per cent different to that terrible day. She was at home on her boat, with her dragon who was now alive! The sun was high in the sky and they were under full sail.

Ever since everyone had moved out of the hotel to live onboard she'd been wanting to do this. But with all the stuff to sort out, this was the first chance they'd had. Well, they could have done it three days ago but school had started again, with live-link classes with Professor Trogalming, their old Boxbury teacher. Because of the time difference Aunt Vera was paying her cash to tutor them in her evenings from her cat-filled flat in London. She was really strict and had given them millions of catch-up exercises to do. Nat still preferred it to having to go back to London.

She heard laughter coming from the upper deck. She turned to find Ah Ping at the wheel in her new "I love San Francisco" t-shirt, chatting to Aunt Vera, who was sitting next to her in Jamuka's old deckchair. Ever since Henry had told her that she looked two hundred years younger with less Cementer on her face, and simpler clothes, her aunt had ditched the mushroom hairdo and packed her designer Shan-xi clothes into one of the *Junko's* storage cupboards.

There'd never been so many people living on the *Junko*. Zixin was snoozing in the hammock hanging from the main mast, and Henry was up at the prow, filming the journey with NutNut.

"*Incoming call again from Wen. D'ya think she's got nothin' else to do?*" said the goat.

"Take it," said Nat.

She was still getting used to the goat handling all her comms. It was so bossy and always had an opinion on everything. It'd been much easier with Fizz. She looked down to where her living, breathing dragon was stretched out on the towel next to her, catching the rays. He was wearing his new, wraparound sunglasses and had his talons wrapped around his very own mouse robot, which had been sent by Philippe.

"Heya, Nat!"

She looked back at the goat. Its silver leaves had knitted together to form a hi-def screen on its back. Wen was jumping up and down on her bed in the middle of a pile of clothes and suitcases.

"Mum's agreed to my master plan. I'm coming to San Francisco. It's so *ding* I'm flying tomorrow. No more school for four weeks! I've got a whole new wardrobe ready and I'm bringing some of those multi-print textron cartridges so we can make you some new things too. No costumes from now on, only functional but *ding* clothes. Do you need anything bringing?"

Nat shook her head. "I don't think I need…"

She didn't get to finish because Fizz hopped up on to her shoulder. "Ahem. Hi Wen, please can you bring Chanko Oyster sauce, Popko Seven Berry juice, and some of that plum cake that your granny makes."

Wen giggled. "Is all that for you?"

He rubbed his tummy. "I'm enjoying trying lots of different food."

She gave him the thumbs-up. "I'll bring you some hot ginger chews as well for your dragon fire."

Fizz made a small bow, and then the three of them started making plans for her visit, which was tricky because every time anyone thought of something the goat waded in. Wen got so irritated she cut the call. Nat had to bite her lip so she didn't giggle. It was going to be an interesting visit.

She got to her feet. They were nearly at the bridge.

"I'm headed up front. Goat, can you go and check in with Aunt Vera about our picnic."

"*Aye, aye,*" it said, trotting off.

Fizz flew up on to her shoulder and she started

making her way across the deck, past Zixin who was snoring in the hammock with Vesperetta draped over his eyes to block out the light.

"Next time you want to call Wen you can use my mouse," whispered Fizz, his snout close to her ear.

"Thanks, that's a *ku* idea! That goat is driving me mad."

Fizz wrapped his wing across the back of her neck. "I was a top robot, wasn't I?"

Nat smiled. "Yes, but you are even better as a real dragon."

Henry lowered NutNut and put him on the rail. "We're making a film of our trip. Professor Trogalming said I'll get a merit if she enjoys it."

Nat patted her cousin on the back. He was fast becoming teacher's pet. They were passing underneath the bridge now. She looked up at the massive orange span above. It was the gateway to San Francisco, the city where her mum had been born. And now it was her home, too.

"Please can we try the sword one more time?" said Henry, taking her hand in his.

She wondered how many more times he'd ask this question before he gave up. Over the last two weeks he'd spent hours in her cabin trying to get it to magic

NutNut into a living, breathing squirrel. She leaned her head against Fizz's chest. His heartbeat was strong and steady. He'd been a one-off robot designed by her dad, holding a ruby secret, but now he was a unique, living dragon whose secret was life itself.